THE MAD LIEUTENANT

LOST PLANET SERIES: BOOK THREE

USA TODAY BESTSELLING AUTHOR

K WEBSTER

NEW YORK TIMES & USA TODAY BESTSELLING AUTHOR

NICOLE BLANCHARD

Mandy,

XOXO

Cover Design: IndieSage
Photo: Shutterstock
Editor: Emily Lawrence
Formatting: IndieSage

CONTENTS

ABOUT THE MAD LIEUTENANT

Her voice brought me back from the darkness, but I don't want the sweet relief she promises. Unlike the rest of the morts on my planet, I don't want a mate. Especially not her.

She's loud, boisterous, and doesn't take no for an answer.

Unlike the rest of the alien females my brothers have woken from cryosleep, Molly doesn't find my growls intimidating. The more I try to ignore her, the more she tries to befriend me.

I'd been taken captive once by the virus that nearly

killed me. I bear its scars, not only on my body, but in my thoughts. No woman, not even one as beautiful as Molly, can heal me.

I don't want her, but she needs me.

THE LOST PLANET SERIES NOTE

In the beginning, there were many who survived the initial blasts of radiation and the resulting catastrophic environmental disturbances. The morts, the only inhabitants of Mortuus, The Lost Planet, ever changed from the effects of the radiation, learned to adapt and, more importantly, to survive. In doing so, they became highly skilled and intelligent, capable of surviving even the worst conditions.

The planet was dangerous, and life wasn't easy, but the morts had each other and that was all that mattered. They flourished in the protective shell of an abandoned building they converted into living quarters. Morts were given jobs, trained from birth in order to pass knowledge from generation to generation.

Eventually, the morts hoped to extend the facility and conquer the wild, untamable outdoors.

Then, disaster struck.

The Rades, a disease contracted from complications of the radiation, began to infect increasing numbers of their population. First, there was fever, followed by sores, then finally madness and, inevitably, death. Quarantining the infected helped, but by then it was too late. Women, children, and the elderly were the first to go. One by one, morts caught The Rades and died. Whole families wiped away.

Until only ten males remained.

Salvation came years later when the morts discovered a ship filled with aliens—female aliens. Knowing it was their only chance at survival, they snuck on a passing ship and brought the females home to study—and to breed.

It was their only chance at survival.

Three females have been claimed. Two remain.

PROLOGUE
DRAVEN

THREE SOLARS LATER

I STEP through the small Decontamination Bay still sizzling from a near miss of a magnastrike. My sub-bones feel as though they're alive and crawling with energy from the blinding white of the magnastrike that melted the back of my suit.

I was nearly rekking killed by the elements, yet it didn't threaten to consume my mind like this facility does. The familiar roaring inside my nog comes raging to the forefront like a pack of hungry sabrevipes eager to feast on my sanity.

Stop thinking about it.

My skin crawls as I quickly dart my gaze back at the exit. I can escape if I need to. I'm not trapped here.

I'm not trapped.

I'm not trapped.

I can escape if I want.

Heat, nothing to do with my near miss with the magnastrike, burns through me. This heat was something that caught fire within me when I'd contracted The Rades. With the fire came the maddening thoughts. The voices. The terror. The darkness. The pain.

Inside my chest, my heart is pounding to the point I feel dizzy. The past three solars, aside from the horrible geostorm, were freeing. When Breccan asked for a volunteer to take Calix and his mate the necessary supplies they needed at Sector 1779, I'd jumped so fast at the chance, I made all the morts around me startle.

This place is a prison.

My mind is a prison.

This rekking planet is a prison.

And despite it all, everyone around me seems happy. Hopeful even. When Theron and Sayer brought back the aliens, it was as though all the morts were brought back to life. As though they had purpose again.

Everyone but me.

The arrival of the females only further aggravated

my mind. Their soft, sweet voices remind me of my mother. Of a past where I once laughed and had purpose. I don't laugh anymore. I don't do anything aside from trying to live solar by solar. The only time I feel some semblance of peace is when I'm in The Tower. And since this geostorm has been ravaging us for nearly a revolution, I haven't spent hardly any time at all up there. This trapped feeling only intensifies each solar.

At one point, I'd looked at the stars beyond and wondered if I could ride with Theron in the *Mayvina*. Maybe the trapped feeling would lessen if I was off this rekking planet. But all that died when the females arrived. They rooted us here. I can see it in Breccan's eyes. He wants to make Mortuus a real home again. Everyone spends countless hours making new plans on how to make our lives better. They look at the future.

I'm stuck in the past.

So often my mind drifts to those dark times when I was captive to that disease. Despite healing from it physically, it has left its wicked mark on my brain. I'll never be free of The Rades. Rekking never.

I'm tearing off my zu-gear as I leave the rigorous cleansing in the small Decontamination Bay when Hadrian saunters up to me, eyes wide and excited.

"The mortyoung is coming! You're just in time!" he bellows. "What did you get?"

His fast talking and energetic movements make me tense. I eye the west entrance door. So close. Ignoring my urge to flee, I reach into my satchel and bring out Calix's notes.

"The supplies Breccan was hoping for do not exist. I searched Sector 1779 myself. However, there are important notes that will be helpful. Plus—"

"We can rekking communicate now thanks to you," he says with a crooked grin. "Females talk a lot. Like a lot. I am thankful Aria has another female to yammer to. Usually Breccan feigns 'work' and leaves me to listen to Aria's never ending tales. She and Emery spoke for nearly half a solar over the smell of a mortyoung's hair." He groans. "Hours and hours, Draven."

Hadrian talks more than either female, so I'm not sure what he's complaining about.

I eye the west entrance door again. It's not too late. I could go back to Sector 1779. It was a little quieter there. The trapped feeling wasn't so bad there.

Boom!

A loud magnastrike makes the entire facility shake, and then we're plunged into total darkness.

I freeze as my heart rate spikes.

I am not trapped. I can escape. Even in the dark. I can get away.

Within seconds, though, everything comes back to life, and we're bathed in light once more. I let out a ragged breath of relief.

Aria's pained scream echoes from what must be Avrell's lab. It reminds me too much of my past—when The Rades consumed my rekking everything.

"Go assist," I bark out. "I'll check to make sure everything stays up and running."

He runs off without another word and disappears into Avrell's lab. Usually Oz or Jareth would handle this sort of thing, but I don't want to be anywhere near a screaming female as she delivers her mortyoung. Rekk no.

Instead, I head in the opposite direction, checking rooms as I go. Everything on the south side of the facility is in working order. I pass Avrell's lab and block out the screaming as I head for the north area of the facility where the females' sub-faction exists. When I get a whiff of an electrical burning, I take off running. Even focused on my task ahead of me, I count doors, exits, windows. I've memorized them all in this facility, yet I can't help but check and double-check. When I reach the source of the smell, I let out a hiss of frustration. The cryochamber room.

Three cryotubes remain. I hate going in this room. Seeing them trapped inside makes me panic. The urge to free them is nearly overwhelming. I don't even like them, but I don't want them trapped. If anyone knows how horrible it feels to be trapped, it's me.

But the last time one was hastily freed, she nearly died. Aria yanked Emery out, and it caused an uproar within our ranks. It was voted that they will remain there, sleeping, until it can be decided on when and how to safely wake them.

Slowly, I walk into the room. Smoke comes from one of the cryotubes. I detach the wires from the standing pod, grab one of the misters, and douse the flames before they can spread.

Pop.

Hiss.

Those two sounds send alarm racing through me. Without thinking, I did exactly what I've been told not to do.

Don't wake them.

I scramble away from the cryotube now that the fire is safely put out and rush to the east door of the cryochamber room. The cool air on the back of my neck—the feel of freedom just behind me—calms me considerably.

I will tell Breccan the geostorm electrical surge caused it.

I will lie.

His warnings to put anyone who messes with the cryotubes into a reform cell has my entire body trembling. When I was eaten up with The Rades, I was forced into one. To protect me from myself. To protect others from me.

I can't go back there.

Not now. Not ever.

Turning, I decide to bolt, but a sound stops me.

Whimpering at first.

Then crying.

Sad, fearful crying.

RUN!

RUNRUNRUNRUN!

Yet my useless boots stay planted to the ground. The lid of the cryotube creaks open. I'm frozen in horror as the alien climbs out of the pod, trembling badly. Her hair is like the other two aliens if you were to mix them together. Light, the color of the sun on top, and dark underneath. It hangs in long, messy waves, covering her breasts. She's not as small as the other two aliens. Her bones are larger. She carries more meat. Maybe this one is stronger. Maybe I haven't hurt her.

Her nog darts all around as she takes in the space, her gaze falling first on the door behind me and then a quick look at the west door behind her. Then, her eyes meet mine. Brown eyes. Wide. Terrified. Spilling liquid. She takes a step toward me, her bottom lip trembling. I take a step back. When she reaches her hand forward, I take another step back.

"H-Help me," she croaks.

She steps forward again and again and again. I stumble back until I crash against the wall beside the door.

Trapped.

My nog darts left and then to just behind her. Exits on two sides of this room.

RUN!

Then her declawed fingers clutch onto my bare arms. All of my minnasuits have been modified to keep my arms free of anything that will touch and chafe my scars. She clings to me, her naked front pressing against me, and I choke on my terror.

I'm trapped.

I'm rekking trapped.

Everything turns black.

I go down, taking the alien with me.

Helpmehelpmehelpme.

Those words are hers or mine or both.

I don't know.

I don't know.

I don't rekking know.

I'm trapped.

"Help me."

This time, I know it's me.

I'm pleading for anyone who will listen.

The black is swirling around me as my world spins. Her breath is hot near my neck, scalding me. Her words mirror mine. The darkness steals me this time, our words echoing back and forth into nothingness.

"Help me."

I'm trapped.

There is no getting away.

This alien will be the death of me.

[1]
MOLLY

The cold is the first thing I notice. At first, I'm confused, then dismayed. Has the power been turned off again? I paid the bill on time. There's no reason why the heat shouldn't be working. Dismay shifts to frustration and anger. I work hard, so hard, to make everything work, but there's always another battle to fight, another catastrophe to avert.

It's my mother's voice that pulls me back from the blues. *"Heavens to Betsy, Molly, it's not the end of the world."*

She'd say that about everything. No problem was too big to conquer for my mother.

Then, I catch the acrid scent of burnt plastic and smoke.

My eyes fly open, but it's not my small apartment

that greets me. The dark room is lit by bright blue lights from standing containers that remind me of the sarcophaguses I'd seen in a magazine once. I was never rich enough to afford to see such fancy things, but I enjoyed looking at the pretty pictures. Inside the windows of the containers opposite me, there are faces of two other slumbering women.

I lift my arm to rub my eyes. What a strange dream! But my hand knocks against a wall. Frowning, I look down and find a length of metal in front of me, blocking my hand. I've never had many phobias, but claustrophobia rockets up on my list of things I never want to try again.

"Hello?" I call out to the women in the tubes across from me. The sound of my voice reverberates throughout my container. Neither of them reacts.

The haze in my head clears, and panic replaces it. Where am I? How did I get here?

I try to push on the door in front of me, but it doesn't budge at first. *That's not good, Molly. Don't panic, don't panic.* I grit my teeth and focus on getting the door open. The surface inside the container is smooth, some sort of cushioned material. At least the bastards who put me here want me to be comfortable. I glance down at my body, noting my nakedness. Well, maybe not so comfortable. *Don't panic.*

With some effort, I'm able to wiggle the door open, but not by much. "Is anyone there?" I try again, hoping the crack in the door will help. None of them move. My heart stutters as it occurs to me that maybe they're dead. I slam my fists against the glass until they're battered, bruised, and trickling blood from split knuckles.

I have to get out of here. I have to.

Despite my best efforts, the tears fall. Fear engulfs me. What if I'm alone here? What if they've already killed everyone I love?

The smell of burnt plastic has me attacking the door with renewed strength, leaving bloody streaks on the impeccable white cushion. I don't know how long I shove and push against the door, but eventually, something *cracks* and the door inches open. Freezing, I think I'm a little shocked it worked. A haze of smoke leaks into the coffin I'm in, and I cough.

It occurs to me as the door begins to creak open that maybe I was safer inside than whatever waits for me outside the safety of the container. My whole body shakes with a combination of fear, adrenaline, and apprehension. I'm incredibly exposed without clothes and alone in a strange place—more vulnerable than I've ever been in my life. I don't want to cry, I hate crying, but I find myself sobbing harder. No amount of my mother's voice calms me down.

I blink rapidly to clear my vision of the tears, but it's no use. They spill out over my cheeks and drip onto my bare stomach. Surveying the strange room, I step out into what looks like a watery grave from the eerie, blue-green light emanating from the strange, coffin-like tubes. My gaze lands on a odd figure. It's massively tall, filling the entire doorway. And pale. Ghostly pale. I'm so focused on getting back home, fear leaves me for a moment.

I take a hesitant step forward. The figure moves back in response. I pause, my brow furrowing. It seems afraid of me, but that can't be right. I stumble a little and reach out my hand. The figure steps back again. Maybe it's confused.

"H-Help me," I say, and my voice sounds like I haven't used it in a thousand years, which strikes me as strange. How long have I been here? Oh God, could it have been days? Or worse, much, much worse, years?

The thought propels my feet forward, and I stumble like a puppet on strings with my near-useless legs. The figure retreats until it's backed against the wall. I continue after it and fall against its body. I cling to its arms to keep my weak body upright. The figure makes a choked sound of surprise, and I begin to babble out pleas. "Help me, please. I don't know where I am or what's going on. Please. I won't hurt you, I promise. I just need to know how to get out of here. How long have I been here? Oh my God. Please help me."

The pleading clears my thoughts and cuts through the panic. Only it's not my own voice I'm hearing, but that of the figure I'm clinging to, who is fighting to pull away from me like my mere touch causes it immeasurable pain.

"Helpmehelpmehelpme," it begs.

It seems to collapse, and I fall with it to the floor, banging my elbow in the process. I'm torn between my natural response to help and my surprise at the gall of this creature, my captor, to beg *me* to help *it*. The anger slices through my sorrow, my tears. I scramble away and to my feet. Without my nearness, it seems to blink away its daze, mimicking my movement.

My vision clears, and I find myself stumbling back from the alien-like being in front of me. My throat closes around the sound of surprise, suppressing it.

He's seven feet tall, possibly taller. Massive in the shoulders and thighs. Hands nearly the size of dinner plates. His size alone would be manageable if it weren't for the ghastly white color of his skin that shines as though it's iridescent. The jet-black color of his closely-cropped hair and opaque, fathomless quality of his dark eyes contrast against the paleness of his skin. A suit made of some sort of rubbery material covers everything but his face, neck, and arms. It reminds me of an insect's exoskeleton.

In short, if I was scared before, the massive *something* standing in front of me increases that tenfold. At least until it appears that he seems more scared of me than I am of him.

I realize this is my chance. I could cower and succumb to the panic and fear, but that won't get me the answers I need to get out of here and go home. I suck back the rest of my tears and take several deep breaths to calm myself.

You got this, girl. You can do this.

"I'm sorry, I didn't mean to scare you." Stepping forward only makes him press back into the wall, so I hold my ground. "I'll help you." The words taste as bitter as the smoke still lingering in the room.

He presses his large hands over those odd eyes and clutches his head as though suffering from an excruciating migraine. Groans rumble in his immense chest, almost lion-like.

Is he hurt? Did whatever cause the fire hurt him, too? From a short distance away, I observe his body for wounds, but aside from hideous scars on his forearms, I don't see any others. Unless they're internal.

I need to calm him down enough to get some answers, so I do the first thing that comes to mind. The same thing I've done to soothe countless times before.

I sing.

First, I hum softly, which seems to calm him somewhat, but he's still shaking and clutching at his head. His sharpened, elongated nails dig into the forgiving flesh of his forearms. I pick the first song that comes to mind and fumble through the words with my unused voice, sounding more like a bull-frog than anything. But it stills his hands.

Singing "I Will Survive" by Gloria Gaynor to an alien has to be the weirdest thing I've ever done.

Slowly, torturously, he begins to calm. His trembling eases, though his legs buckle, and he nearly collapses again. When the song ends, I restart it because I'm afraid if I do anything else, my own panic will come back. I go through it three more times before his eyes find mine again, and his hands clench by his sides, still. Blood oozes from his arms, dripping onto the floor between us.

I slowly approach him, softly crooning the last lines of the song. "Are you all right?" I dare to ask.

In answer, he shoots away from me, and after

waving his arm at a sensor, he causes the door inlaid into the wall beside him to spring open. He disappears out the door. I'm confused for a moment but jump to attention and dart through the opening before I'm locked outside of wherever he's going.

I find myself in an empty hallway lit by red, flashing lights. Someone screams nearby, which doesn't help my level of panic. The tall guy completely disappears around the corner. When I hear voices, I rush after him, almost running right into two other aliens who exit from a different room. They gape at me. I wonder why everyone is so damned surprised to see *me*.

One of the new aliens has long, black hair, longer than mine, and it's twisted into one of those man buns—which is so weird, yet oddly familiar—on top of his head. In his arms, he holds a stack of books. The other reminds me of a mad scientist. His hair shoots up in all directions, and he's sporting bandages on several of his fingers. They both dart their gazes where the other one ran off to before looking back at me.

"Mortarekker," says the one with the man bun. "Did Draven finally lose what was left of his mind? I swear he was running *from* her."

The mad scientist tilts his head, those strange, black eyes observing me. "I don't doubt it. He can barely stand his own company, and he doesn't want a mate."

Mate?

He glances toward the room with the containers and repeats the strange word the first said. "Looks like the magnastrike caused the cryotube to malfunction."

The first puts the books down on the floor beside him then shrugs out of his jacket. "We were due to wake up another, but Breccan won't be pleased."

"Breccan has other worries at the moment," says the crazy haired dude.

The two of them speak to each other so quickly and with such familiarity, I wonder if they're brothers or maybe best friends.

I wrap myself in book-guy's rubbery jacket which is long enough it goes down to my knees. "Thank you," I say. None of them have tried to hurt me, but I make sure to keep my guard up. The book-guy's smile is so open and inviting, I want to relax and smile back, but not until I have more answers. "Please, will you explain? Why am I here? What's going on?"

Book-guy wraps an arm around my shoulders, and they both turn and lead me down the hallway they came from. "That's a long story..."

"Molly," I supply. "Molly Franklin."

"Molly. I'm Sayer, and this is Jareth."

I nod to Jareth. "You aren't—you aren't going to h-hurt me, are you?"

Sayer squeezes my arm. "We're not going to hurt you. We'd never hurt a female." He sounds offended at the thought. "Right, Uvie?"

"Affirmative," a computerized voice chirps from a speaker above us, startling me.

"Can you tell me where I am?" Maybe then I won't feel as disconcerted.

"You're on the planet Mortuus. We are its last remaining inhabitants."

My stomach clenches in emptiness. I lift a hand to my head, wondering if I'm going to swoon. "I'm on another planet? H-how did I get here?" I'm also curious about the other alien I'd encountered, but one thing at a time.

"It's best that we let Avrell or Breccan explain things to you," Sayer says.

Jareth snorts. "Not likely. They're both busy at the moment." A scream punctuates his statement.

I jump, and Sayer rubs my arm. "What was that?" I envision someone being tortured.

"Our commander's mate is giving birth to a morty-oung," Sayer answers.

"Don't worry, she was always a loud one," Jareth adds.

This answer is almost worse than someone being tortured, but I switch topics. “There are other women here? Like the ones in the containers?”

The two nod. “We came upon several alien females, and as our numbers are so few, it was decided we would mate with the females to continue our population,” Jareth explains.

I push that thought away, too.

I’m on another planet, trapped with aliens who want to use me to breed.

Great.

[2]
DRAVEN

I RUSH to throw on my zu-gear, desperate for an escape. Unlike the clingy material of my minnasuit, the zu-gear doesn't bother my itchy arms. I push through the doors that lead to the stairwell that goes to The Tower. I need space. I need to see the vastness of our planet and remind myself I'm not trapped.

I'm not.

Before I take my first step of ascent, I snag a gnarly looking magknife off the weapons wall. You don't go to The Tower unless you're armed. With the zuta-metal handle tight in my grip, I start climbing the steep stairs. Sometimes, I run as fast as I can to the top. It's liberating, and for a few moments, my mind is free from dark, soul-shredding clutter.

Up and up and up, I climb the hundreds of steps.

When I reach the outer door that takes me into The Tower that overlooks Mortuus, I take a deep breath, hating that I have to suck in the hot recycled air inside my mask. Just once I wish I could pull the mask off and breathe in the planet's air.

But with freely breathing, I'd be inviting those toxins back into my bloodstream. Toxins and pathogens that already nearly destroyed me once. When I contracted The Rades, I barely survived. Despite the maddening inside my mind, I can't help but cling desperately to this life.

I crave more than freedom, fresh air, and an escape from the crushing thoughts that assault me each solar.

I crave happiness.

My mind is elsewhere when I push through the heavy zuta-metal door. Because of the horrendous geostorm, I have to hold onto the handrails to keep from being shot out one of the windows and into the winds of the storm. With a groan of frustration, I grab one of the harnesses attached to the wall and reluctantly bind myself to it. As much as I love my freedom, I'm not stupid. One false move and I could be swept into The Eternals. My bones would be left out somewhere in The Graveyard for the vicious sabrevipes to feed on.

No rekking thank you.

Something heavy thuds down on the floor nearby, and I squint my eyes, searching for the offender. Up here, everything is an offender. Mostly, it's the armworms you have to watch out for. When the weather is harsh, they like to seek shelter in *my* shelter.

Gripping my magknife in one hand and holding onto the handrail with the other, I circle around the observation deck to the back side that's hidden from me. Just like I assumed, a pair of armworms is crawling around, hissing and spitting venom.

It's been many micro-revolutions since I've been able to bring Avrell any armworms. He uses the venom for medicinal purposes. With quick movements, despite the raging winds that have sand pinging the glass of my mask, I charge the larger of the armworms. The other seems to be the female, looking to nest. My magknife comes down hard, and I pierce the male armworm through its head, pinning it to the ground. It squirms as the life drains from it. The female realizes I'm a threat and slithers toward me. Its middle is swollen with eggs. I'll need to be careful not to destroy them. Even though the armworms are terrible for eating, a female armworm's eggs taste rekking delicious.

The creature hisses at me, aiming its sharp teeth for my leg, but having dealt with these things for many revolutions, I anticipate its movement. With a slam of my boot, I stomp on its head. Guts splatter out on either side of my boot. This one's venom is gone now, but the eggs are safe. I set to grabbing a decontamination bag then push the carcasses into it. I leave it in a heap by the door and then walk over to my favorite spot.

The northerly wind nearly knocks me over, so I hold on with both hands and lean into it. Magnastrikes are lighting up the red-orange storm clouds. Everywhere. This storm is one of the worst we've seen, but my gut tells me it'll let up soon. Normally, I can see Lake Acido just beyond the mountain, but not this solar. Currently, I can barely see past the length of my arm beyond The Tower openings.

I hear another sound behind me, and I whip around, ready to take out more armworms. When I see another mort hooking himself to a harness, I let out a groan. This is usually my private space.

My comms unit within my suit crackles to life as whoever my visitor is comes near. He grabs hold of the handrail beside me and shakes his head.

"You're such an odd rekking mort standing out here in the middle of our history's worst geostorm," Jareth says.

I snort. "Did you come here to insult me?"

He shakes his head. The wind whistles between us, making it difficult to hear his words. "I came to talk sense into that nog of yours."

Sense?

"I don't understand," I grumble.

"The female."

I tense at his words. "The magnastrike set her cryotube on fire. It wasn't my fault."

He chuckles. "I rekking know that. You of all morts would not willingly go against Breccan's orders, much less free some beautiful female alien just for joy. That's much more Hadrian or Theron. Not you, Draven."

"Your point?"

He turns slightly to face me. "You need to claim her."

Disgust coils in the pit of my stomach like an armworm in a nest. "I will not."

"You should."

"Why?" I demand, fury rolling through my every nerve ending.

"Because someone else will." He pauses. "And you found her. You deserve her."

Imagining the female with Hadrian or Theron has more anger rippling through me. I don't rekking care...

So why am I ready to knock the rogshite out of one of those two?

"I prefer to be alone. Let someone else have her." I narrow my eyes at him. "You?"

He shifts his eyes away. "I don't want her."

"Sayer?"

"He doesn't want her either," he snaps sharply at me.

We both grow quiet. For a moment, I feel a pang of protectiveness over her. Why do they not want her? Because she is more solidly built than Emery or Aria? Are these morts so insecure that they need a fragile mate to feel better about themselves?

"She was chasing after you when we found her," Jareth says with a sigh. "This one is much friendlier than the other two were. Healthy, too. I think, perhaps, she found comfort in you somehow."

I snarl from behind my mask. She made me a weak, blubbering mess. Her simple, harmless touch sent me hurtling into the madness of my mind.

But then...

I try to ignore the memory.

I will survive.

Somehow, sweetly spoken words that felt like they moved and tickled my skin dragged me from the vast void inside my nog. When I came back to, I fled from her. A shudder ripples down my spine.

"Think about it," he says. "Now come on. I'll help you get the armworms decontaminated."

"Careful," I tell him, ignoring his earlier words over about the female altogether. "The female armworm has eggs in her."

He makes a loud sound of excitement before grabbing up the bag. We make our way back inside, the crushing, trapped feeling when I'm indoors nearly suffocating me. Just inside the doors, we step into a mini decontamination stall and take the time to clean off our suits first. Then, we wash the armworms before transferring them to a sterile bag. We exit the decontamination stall and carry on our way. The descent is filled with Jareth's voice as he talks about some book Sayer is working on. I'm only half listening.

My mind is back on the female.

"Molly."

I look at him in confusion as he pulls off his mask at the bottom of the stairs. "What is this strange word?"

He laughs, baring his double fangs at me. "It's her name, mortarekker. Your mate."

I growl as I yank off my mask. "She is not my mate. Take care of that tongue, or I'll take care of it for you."

"Oooh, I'm rekking terrified," he says, feigning fear. It makes me want to thump him right between his eyes.

"Leave my presence, pest."

He snorts. "You're lucky we're trapped here with you. Otherwise you wouldn't have any friends."

His choice of words has my sub-bones cracking in my neck and my ears flattening against my nog. The smile falls from his mouth as he realizes his misstep, and I relax once more.

"Enough with the amusement," he says, growing serious. "Remember what I said about Molly. She needs a good mate. Someone who doesn't want to use her to breed like a rogcow. As much as I'm looking forward to our race thriving again, I don't think the same way as Breccan. He may be our commander, but he sometimes gets so set in his ways. Molly needs friends, not five morts hovering over her just waiting for her to bend over so they can spurt their seed in her."

I whirl around, fury rising up so quick I swear my vision turns crimson. "They threaten to take her against her will?" The roar that erupts from me vibrates off the walls.

He flinches and quickly shakes his nog. "N-No, Draven. I'm only saying they want her for a mate."

As I follow him through the doors and we shed our zu-gear, I can't help but replay his words. Five morts. Not myself. Not Breccan or Calix as they already have mates. And not Sayer and Jareth. Because they don't want mates either for some reason.

Hadrian, Galen, Oz, Avrell, and Theron.

Hadrian may be the youngest mort, but I see the way his eyes linger on Breccan and Aria, jealousy flickering in them. Galen, our faction's botanist, always seems to be sneaking peeks at the females. Ozias may have his nog down tinkering on his projects, being he's our mechanical engineer, but I've watched him on more than one occasion licking his lips whenever Aria is near, his projects easily forgotten. Theron, our rekking crazy pilot and navigator of the *Mayvina*, has been quite vocal about taking a mate. And then there's Avrell. He may be our doctor and looks after the health of these alien females, but I've felt the longing coming from him in waves. I know he desperately craves a mate.

I stride past Jareth down the corridor on a path to anywhere but near him and his maddening words until voices in the sub-faction have me halting. Jareth chuckles as he passes with our bag of armworms. Ignoring him, I peek my head into the sub-faction. The new female—Molly—sits on the lounger in the middle of the room with Sayer at her side and with Oz and Galen standing nearby. Both Oz and Galen seem enraptured by whatever it is she's saying. I watch as she speaks with her hands. Big gestures. Wild movements. And she doesn't even need to use them because her voice...

She's so loud.

The constant buzz inside my nog is silenced because her unusual, boisterous voice drowns it out. She's no longer naked but instead now wears a minnasuit that is tight on her chest. I'm struck, staring at how the material seems to hug her breasts. It's then I realize both Oz and Galen are admiring her there, too.

Molly needs friends, not five morts hovering over her just waiting for her to bend over so they can spurt their seed in her.

A growl of protectiveness bellows from me, yanking all their attention my way. The cool, open air of the doorway behind me keeps me calm. With the most threatening glare I can muster, I tell Oz and Galen wordlessly to back off.

She's mine.

The thought has me pausing.

I don't want her for a mate.

I simply want to protect her from those who want to mate with her.

"Leave," I bark out. I am second-in-command at the facility, and I'm not afraid to use my position over them.

Sayer snorts, and Molly lets out a huff.

"Rude much?" she grumbles.

Snapping my eyes to hers, I check her over to make sure she is not distressed. If anything, she looks fairly comfortable. Far more comfortable than Emery or Aria ever were. Her brown eyes assess me with a mixture of curiosity and annoyance.

Not fear.

Not like earlier when I inadvertently let her out of her cryotube.

"I was just bringing her a gift," Galen says as he sets down a bag filled with what I know are goldenroot candies.

Pop. Pop. Pop.

One by one, my sub-bones crack in my neck as I rise to my full, intimidating height. I have twenty-eight sub-bones, and I crack them slowly, my eyes full of fury as I glower at Galen. My ears flatten so tight against my nog I can hardly hear anything besides the burning rage roaring inside me.

Goldenroot candies are something he created for the humans. For when Breccan was trying to please his mate. Is Galen trying to please Molly?

Galen slinks away wisely, but Oz's attention is still on Molly. He holds out a zuta-metal necklace. Another gift the female aliens are known to enjoy.

Pop. Pop. Pop. Pop. Pop. Pop. Pop. Pop. Pop. Pop. Pop. Pop. Pop. Pop. Pop. Pop. Pop. Pop. Pop. Pop. Pop. Pop. Pop. Pop.

Oz nearly trips over his own feet when he realizes I'm approaching and snarling. Our eyes meet as my final sub-bone cracks into place.

Pop.

"We were just leaving," Galen says, grabbing Oz's arm and dragging him away.

Turning my body, I shoot my vicious stare at Sayer. Instead of scrambling away, he grins at me.

"We were just explaining to Molly about our planet's future. Our race's future."

"Leave," I bellow.

The piece of rogshite doesn't flinch a muscle. "I'm not a threat, Draven. I don't want to mate with Molly."

Molly.

Finally, my attention turns back to her. Her brown eyes twinkle with amusement, and then she starts laughing. Laughing and laughing. And laughing.

I blink at her in confusion.

Maybe I found another being on this retched planet who's just as mad as me.

And as much as that should terrify me, it doesn't.

Rekk, why doesn't it?

She's mine.

I don't want to mate with her!

But protecting her gives me a feeling of purpose. Something I haven't felt in more revolutions than I can remember. I will keep her safe from Oz and Galen. And that empty-nog Hadrian. Avrell is no threat to me, even though I am sure he would love to have a mate. But Theron is. He's the one who procured these females in the first place. He may think he has ownership over my Molly.

Over my dead rekking body.

[3]
MOLLY

At Draven's harsh words, the rest of my visitors exit the door, leaving me alone with the imposing alien who still looks as though he'd like to eat me alive. Being someone's dinner is most definitely *not* on my bucket list.

"You didn't have to scare them away," I chastise. "We were just getting to know each other."

His nostrils flare, and his neck cracks ominously. "You have no need to get to know them," he answers.

"Oh, honey," I say with a dismissive wave of my hand, "I may have been brought here against my will, but that don't mean I have to be inhospitable. That's just bad manners. Besides, aside from you, the other aliens have been downright gentlemen."

"Morts are not gentle," he growls. "And *you* are the alien."

I hold the curious necklace the one named Oz gave me out for inspection. I've always had an affinity for pretty things. Gesturing to Draven, I say, "Isn't this just *darling*?" Sounds of pleasure escape my chest. "The others have been explaining to me about how I ended up here. I have to say, I was as nervous as a cat in a room full of rocking chairs at first, let me tell you. I mean, you have to agree it was a shock." I chuckle a little as I turn the necklace this way and that. "I think we both may have given each other quite a scare. I may still be a little out of it, but I pinched myself hard enough to give me a heck of a bruise, so I guess it can't be a nightmare." I'm babbling, I always babble, but I can't seem to stop. "Sayer explained about your race and the disease. I just can't even imagine. Bless your hearts."

"Sayer explained," Draven says through gritted teeth, "about needing a mate?"

I lift a shoulder dismissively and clasp the necklace around my neck. "He did. I haven't quite wrapped my head around it all yet. How could I? But they were very kind. Is this candy?" Before he can answer, I pop one into my mouth. The sugar-sweetness bursts over my tongue, causing me to make a sound of pleasure.

"Mmmm! This is just like butterscotch. Well, don't that just beat all?"

"What else did they explain about mates?" Draven takes a step closer. I eye him warily. I haven't quite decided if he's dangerous or not. He doesn't seem as unstable as he did when we first met, but there's still a wild energy around him that reminds me of an untamed animal—like the first provocation will send him nipping and kicking at anyone in his immediate vicinity. I'd rather not be there when that happens.

"Sayer and Jareth brought me to the sub-faction—Is that the right term?—Anyway, they told me how you are the last of your kind, that you found me and the others, and have decided to take us as mates among you. How does that work—exactly? Are we assigned one of you?" My tone is blithe and uncaring. Better to get the harsh realities over with as soon as possible, so I can deal with them. I've never quite been in *this* situation, but I've dealt with life-altering changes before, and I will deal with this, too.

I have to.

As I wait for his answer, I begin to hum another tune. This one is "I Walk the Line" by Johnny Cash. Draven reminds me a bit of Johnny Cash. Rough around the edges. A rule-breaker. If his scars and brash demeanor are any indication, he's not the gift-giving kind like the others. Not that it matters. I haven't decided which alien I'll let woo me, for now, but Draven doesn't seem like the mating sort.

The sliding door behind him opens, and another alien—one I haven't met yet—walks through, his pace brisk and no-nonsense. He's draped in a thin gown over his suit—like the one I'm wearing—except his is covered in smears of blood. Draven snaps to attention, his ears flattening, and long, dangerous looking claws extend from his massive hands.

"Aria?" Draven barks at the newcomer.

With a sigh of relief the other alien says, "She's well. All is well. Their son is also. They've named him Sokko, after Breccan's father."

I freeze, the butterscotch-like candy sticking in my throat. My tongue seems to have swollen in size, and I wonder if I'll choke on them both. The two aliens don't seem to notice my distress.

"A son," Draven says, almost breathlessly. "A son."

A baby. There's a baby here.

"Yes, it's incredible. But first, Breccan was wondering what the alarms were earlier. He sent me to check. Is everything—"

It's then he notices me. I lift a hand in welcome, swallowing the last of the candy, even though it scratches my throat on the way down. "Hey there," I say with what I hope is a friendly smile. "I'm Molly."

"Mortarekker," the new alien says. "What is the meaning of this?" he demands of Draven. "Breccan will have your nog for waking a female early. We were supposed to wait until Calix returned to run more tests. Aria's delivery was successful, but we still don't know if that will always be the case. How could you be so reckless?"

As the other alien berates Draven, I watch as Draven's ears press closer and closer to his skull. The slits of his eyes pinch closed until only the barest glint of black is visible. I'm reminded of a puppy I once owned when I was a girl. The poor dear had been abused by her previous owner, and even though she was only a few months old, she'd already learned to make herself as small as possible whenever she encountered loud sounds. What had happened to Draven to make him react the same way?

I launch myself to my feet and across the room before I know what I'm doing. "It wasn't his fault!" I interrupt. "The other ones—Sayer and Jareth—they told me a magna-something hit the building and fried the thingy I was in. It made it malfunction, and Draven saved me." Save is a loose interpretation of what he did, and I expect him to interject, but he's quiet behind me. I can feel the waves of anxious energy buffeting against my back. He's practically vibrating. "It wasn't his fault," I repeat firmly.

The alien in front of me purses his lips. Despite his harsh words toward Draven, he doesn't seem like the malicious type. His eyes—black though they are—seem kind. His fangs aren't sharp and imposing like the others, they've been filed down to look somewhat normal. He holds up a hand, which I clasp with my own, and gives me a benevolent smile.

"Forgive me," he says, "I did not mean to frighten you. My name is Avrell. I'm what you would call a doctor here at the facility. You're...Molly, you said?"

My shoulders slump in relief. "That's right."

"Why don't you come with me? Breccan and Aria could use some time to bond with their mortling before the others demand to shower them with well wishes. While they rest, I should do some tests on you." At my horrified look, Avrell hurries to explain, "Don't worry, standard procedure. Since your cryotube was damaged, we'd be remiss to neglect an exam. If you'll follow me." He gestures to the doorway he came through.

I hesitate. "Do you mind if Draven comes with me?" The only reason I manage to lock my arm around Draven's before he can escape is because I catch him off guard. Any one of the other guys would throw themselves at my feet to go with me, but Draven is the only one who would rather be anywhere else—which is exactly why I want him. As much as I enjoy their attention, Draven won't expect anything from me. In fact, I can guarantee that as soon as he's able, he'll be running in the other direction.

And I'm counting on it.

***

I hiss as Avrell helps me onto the cool surface of the table. My eyes are clenched tightly. "How long will it take?" I ask, trying to keep my teeth from chattering. It's not the cold that's making me shiver. It's fear. Fear worse than waking up in a strange place, trapped.

"We implanted all the females once we transferred them safely to the facility," Avrell explains. Am I mistaken or was there a thread of apology in his voice?

"Did—" I grit my teeth, then force myself to calm down. "Did any of them take?" *Please say no. Please say no.* I'll worry about the injustice of being implanted against my will later. Can't think about that now.

There's a pause punctuated by the sound of fingers against a keyboard, then I feel the blunt head of some sort of scanner against the lower portion of my belly. Avrell had me change into a thin gown for the general health exam—which I passed with flying colors—then he had me sit on an exam table with a blanket on my lap with the gown pulled up over my belly.

"I apologize for this dated technology, but the wegloscan is under maintenance. Oz is adding some new features to it," Avrell mutters. "For now, we must run this test the old way."

Weglo-what?

As he continues, I try not to think about Draven staring at me in such a vulnerable position. He'd come with me to Avrell's office and exam room—grudgingly. The moment we'd stepped over the threshold, he'd taken up residence in a corner of the room, crossed his arms over his chest, and hadn't stopped glowering since.

"Did any of them take?" I ask again, my voice growing shrill.

"We're not certain," Avrell finally answers. "The first embryo we implanted in Aria, Commander Breccan's mate, didn't take," Avrell continues as he positions the wand in different locations on my stomach. "We're still not sure why. Propagating a species, even same species, is a delicate process. Cross-species, well, I'm not going to say it's impossible, but it takes time."

"But I thought you said they just had a baby?" My throat closes around the word.

"They did, but their mortling was conceived—ah, in the more conventional sense."

My cheeks burn even though my eyes are closed. "Right! Well, of course." So, if I wasn't pregnant, I was going to have to have sex with one of them. No wonder they were all giving me gifts. In the abstract sense, I understood what they'd meant when they said they wanted me as a mate. It just didn't sink in until now.

Next to me, Avrell gives a disappointed sigh. Unbidden, my eyes fly open and my gaze darts to the screen. The visual there isn't that much different from the ultrasounds where I'm from, and it doesn't take a doctor like Avrell to tell me what I already know.

I'm not pregnant.

For some reason, I glance in Draven's direction. He's also studying the screen with an intensity that makes the hair on my arms stand on end. What is he thinking about? Then his gaze meets mine.

I don't need fancy gifts from Draven.

All it takes is a look.

The raw emotion in his eyes reaches down deep inside me where I'm empty and wanting, taking root.

He shakes his head, taking a step back. I know he feels it, whatever it is, because he meets my gaze once more then shakes his head again, slowly. Whatever he sees in my expression, he's telling me no.

"No matter," Avrell says blithely. "Like I said, it's a delicate process. This will give us time to test your compatibility with each mort and find the best viable candidate. We really should have done this with the others, but circumstances being what they were, we never got the chance." Avrell looks up from the screen where he is recording data and finds Draven staring at me. "Oh," Avrell says.

"Doctor," I say, turning to Avrell, who is glancing back and forth between Draven and me with a frown pulling at his lips. "Wouldn't you say reproduction is more successful with willing mates? In humans, it's been beneficial for the couple to be in a happy, healthy relationship before procreating. Don't you think the same would be true in our case?"

"I—don't follow," Avrell says haltingly.

"If I'm going to be required to have a mate, to give them a child, don't you think it's only fair that I get a say in the matter?"

Avrell leans forward, panic in his eyes. "Now, Molly, the science of it all—"

"I don't give a fig about science. You brought me here against my will. I recognize your position, but it was against my will," I say before he can object. "Successful conception would be more easily attained if I were on board with the whole thing. A *willing* mate, if you catch my drift. Either you let me pick my mate, or I'll do everything in my power to thwart your attempts."

My shoulders heave from how hard I'm breathing. Avrell looks as though he wants to throw his fancy clipboard and wand-scanner into the air. Draven hasn't looked at me since I announced I wanted to choose my own mate.

"I'm fearing we may have gotten ourselves in over our nogs," Avrell says, and relief fills me at the humor in his voice. "Who knew aliens would be so much trouble?"

"So, we have a deal?"

Avrell sighs. "I'm willing to propose the option to the commander. Did you have a mate in mind?"

I meet Draven's eyes and nod in his direction. "Him."

[4]
DRAVEN

I REKKING THINK NOT!

My panicked eyes leave the alien, who seems so sure of her choice... Of all morts, she chose *me.* The broken one. The damaged one. The one The Rades nearly destroyed. I find Avrell frowning at me. He's disappointed in her choice. Probably because he wishes she chose *him.*

Unwanted images of him with his filed down teeth near her golden flesh has a growl of warning rumbling from me. I clutch onto a table to keep from doing something horrible like rip his rekking throat out.

Plink! Plink! Plink! Plink! Plink!

I stare down in confusion as I realize my claws have punctured the zuta-metal table in my fury. When I snap my stare up to Avrell, his expression has changed. The disappointment is gone, and determination has settled in his black orbs.

Does he want to challenge me?

Before I can unhook myself from the table, he holds his palms up.

"Stand down, Lieutenant," he says in a calm voice that usually works to get my mind sorted. "Aria wants the female aliens to have choices. This is her choice."

I'm drawn back to the brown eyes of Molly. She, too, wears determination in her expression. Something sad flickers in her stare, but she quickly masks it with a bright smile.

Emery and Aria never smile like that.

Not toward me.

Not toward anyone.

I'm stunned for a moment, warmed by her smile. Is this how Breccan feels when he stands in front of the big windows in the command center letting the UV rays burn into his flesh? Her smile doesn't burn me, though. A thundering inside my chest has me gasping for breath. So many solars my heart would race to the point of pain. This feels different. Controllable.

I have control.

Once I've calmed myself, I try to smile back. Testing it out on my lips. Both she and Avrell cringe. It makes me wonder if I showed too much fang. Quickly, I chase it away with a scowl.

"I don't want a mate," I utter to them.

Avrell sighs. "I know, but as Lieutenant, there are certain duties expected of you. Consider this one of them." With those words, he exits the room.

Molly slowly approaches me the same way I sneak up on armworms, but instead of running a magknife through my nog, she gently grips my wrist.

"Listen, buddy-o," she says in her bright voice that lights up dark shadows inside of me.

Buddy-o?

"I'm gonna be real straight with you," she says. "My life was giant pile of manure before I woke up here. Huge pile. Stunk to high heaven."

I frown, cocking my nog to try to make sense of her words.

"Things are a little blurry, but the important parts are still there," she tells me, tapping the side of her nog with her finger. "This Star Wars planet is a total step up for me. Like sweet baby Jesus was throwing me a bone. Lord, did I ever need a bone."

I'm blinking rapidly at her because she may as well be ronking like a rogcow. I don't understand any of what she means. "You want a bone?" I thought Oz was the only one who liked to chew on the beasts' bones after the meat has been cleaned off.

"Keep up, Alien Scissorhands." She gestures at the scars on my arms as if this explains her words. "Anyway, all I'm saying is we're in this boat together. We can either sink or swim. I've always been afraid of drowning. So, this whole mating gig? It's our oar. We can take turns and do our part. Coast along."

She makes an exaggerated effort to bob her nog up and down.

I mimic her action because her expectant eyes plead for me to.

"Whew!" she cries out. "I was sure you were going to turn me down, and I'd have to take that Sayer guy. He was nice—"

A loud growl rattles in my chest, stopping her words.

"Oh, you'll do, honey," she says, flashing me another one of her brilliant, sunny smiles. "You have that intimidation thing down pat. We can look out for each other. I'll make sure they leave you alone about this whole mating business, and you can make sure no one tries to mate with me."

"If they touch you, I will rip their limbs from their bodies," I snarl, overcome with a fierce need to protect this babbling alien.

"Okay, Rambo. You're getting a little too into the part. We're just going to act. Understand?"

I think back to the time Hadrian made me "act" as though I were Breccan and he was Aria. To please Aria for the commander. Aria calls it a movie. I know how to "act."

"I understand," I say slowly. "We will not physically mate." I refuse to look at the manuals explaining how mating is performed. The idea of someone touching me without my minnasuit between us makes my skin itch. Absently, I claw at my forearm.

"Right," she agrees. "We just tell them we do." Her eyes drop to where I'm scratching my arm, and she stops me with a gentle touch. "We'll protect each other."

"I don't need protecting," I growl.

Her smile falls and her brows bunch together. I don't like when her eyes look sad. "I think you do. Your monsters are just different than mine."

What monsters does she possess?

The door opens, and Hadrian pokes his nog in. "Commander says—rogshite!" His eyes roam over *my mate* and hunger gleams in them. My growl of warning is fierce as I step in front of her, shielding her from his stare.

"Mine," I snarl.

His features fall, and he looks as though he might drop to the floor kicking and screaming like he used to do when he was a little mortling. Instead, he straightens his back. "I'm Hadrian. You must be Draven's mate," he addresses her, his voice dry. "Everyone is visiting the mortling. Come on. They're expecting you."

He stalks off, clearly envious over the fact that Molly is my mate. Pride thumps inside my chest. She's a mate in name only. It brings me great relief that I won't be expected to do more.

"Come," I bark out to my mate.

She grabs my bicep, stopping me. "I-I can't."

Turning, I look at her over my shoulder. Her brown eyes are watery as though they may leak at any moment. My mouth waters. Breccan wrote in explicit details in the alien manual about the sweet taste of their tears. It makes me curious.

"I, uh, I don't want to see it," she mutters. "Can't we like go hang out at your place? Take a nap? Shoot the breeze? Count freaking stars for all I care?"

"You want to go to The Tower?"

She nods rapidly. "Sure. Take me there."

Indecision wars within me. As much as that idea intrigues me, I refrain from doing just that. Hadrian was sent by my commander to take me to view the mortling. So, view it we will.

"Not now," I bite out. I storm out of the room, and the sound of her bare feet slapping the floors behind me is the only indication she's following. I stride through the facility on a hunt for Breccan and Aria. We follow the sounds of excited voices until we are at the doorway of Breccan's chambers.

"Draven is here," Hadrian says from within the chambers.

Breccan calls for me. But as I enter, I realize my alien remains rooted to the floor just outside of the room. I cock my nog in confusion.

"Come, mate."

She shakes her head, backing up farther into the hallway. "I'm good right here."

"The commander wants to look at your face," I tell her. "And we are to see the mortling."

Her face pales, and she swallows. "Please don't make me."

Make her?

The panic in her brown eyes reminds me of my own when I'm trapped in a room full of morts. Does she share this same fear as me? I step closer to her and peer down at her. "I will never make you do anything that hurts you."

She tilts her head up bravely. "That will hurt me."

This, I understand.

"Stay, mate," I instruct.

"Molly."

"I know."

Her eyes roll in that annoyed way Aria does often. "I'm saying you should call me Molly, not mate. It's so alpha."

"Breccan is the alpha," I state.

"Oh, Jimminy Christmas! Never mind. Go see the...thing. I'll be right here."

I give her a slow nod, confused at her words yet again, before turning and pushing into the room. The other morts move out of the way to give me my space. I stand in the middle of the room, face-to-face with Breccan.

I've never seen him smile like this, showing all his teeth like he's succumbed to the madness of The Rades. Something moves in his arms, and I tense. My eyes drop to the bundle. As soon as I see the thing, my chest hurts. Why does it hurt? The thing is no mortling I know of. It's different.

Furry black hair like its father.

Speckles on its tiny nose like its mother.

It opens its eyes, and those too are like Breccan's.

But then my eyes travel along its exposed flesh that has a pink hue like Aria's.

Breccan lets out a chuckle. "Sokko has claws like me. See?" He pulls the mortling's hand from inside the bundle. "And these? These are mine." His finger pushes back the dark hair on its nog to reveal flat ears like all morts have. "His tongue is like Aria's, fat and useless."

"Hey," Aria grumbles from the bed. She's paler than usual and appears to be exhausted, but she's smiling happily. "You didn't call my tongue useless the other day."

Breccan growls, and the mortling startles. I take a step back in case the thing jumps out of that bundle at me.

"Can it speak?" I ask.

Several morts laugh nearby, and I feel ashamed by my question.

Breccan doesn't ridicule me, he simply shakes his head. "Not yet. Like morts, alien young don't speak until nearly a whole revolution has passed." His thumb pulls down the tiny creature's chin. "But look at this." Tiny fangs barely puncture the otherwise toothless gums.

"It is unusual," I utter.

"I think you meant the most beautiful thing you have ever seen," Aria chides.

I don't open my mouth to argue, but the most beautiful thing I've seen is my mate. I may not want to touch her, but I enjoy looking at her. Especially her mouth.

"Your sub-bones," Breccan says, dragging me from my inner thoughts.

"About that," Avrell says. "Molly has chosen Draven as her mate."

Aria sits up and gapes. "She chose someone? Already? We barely got word that the cryotube malfunctioned, and we have a new human here, yet you're telling me she's already chosen someone?" She scoffs and points at Hadrian. "Bring her in."

Before I can stop him, Hadrian is out the door. Molly's distressed scream pierces the air. Like a contagion, the mortling in Breccan's arms wails in response. I become focused only on getting to my mate, slinging morts out of the way as I charge to get back to her in the hallway. When I see Hadrian's hands on her shoulders as he attempts to guide her toward the room, I lose my rekking mind.

"DO NOT TOUCH MY MATE!" I bellow, yanking a magknife from my belt along the way toward him.

Hadrian's eyes grow wide in shock as I raise my arm, ready to send him to The Eternals for hurting my mate. I promised her I would protect her. I've already failed, and we've barely established that she is to be mine. Before I can smash the sharp tip into his skull, someone strong grabs my arm and jerks me back. Jareth.

"What are you doing?" he hisses, wrestling the magknife out of my grip. As soon as he takes it from me, he lets go of my arm.

Hadrian has wisely removed his hands from Molly. As soon as she's free, she rushes over to me. Her spindly arms wrap around my middle. I freeze as terror claws up my spine. Last time she grabbed me like this, I succumbed to the darkness. But now? Now, the urge to gut Hadrian keeps me drawn into the light. To protect her.

"Thank you," she murmurs, her hot breath tickling my chest over my minnasuit.

I bring my nostrils to the hair on her nog and inhale. My eyes remain locked on Hadrian in warning. He glowers back but stays far away from me.

"This is your wish, little one?" Breccan asks, no longer holding the mortling. "You wish to mate with Draven?"

She nods but refuses to look at him. "Yes. Now can

we please leave? I'm tired. We can talk about all this later."

Breccan frowns at me. He knows me better than any mort here. He knows I don't want to mate. Not at all. My commander is intelligent, and I can see the questions dancing in his eyes. For now, all he does is nod his approval. It's enough for me. I pry the alien away from me, giving us much needed space, and point next door to where my chambers are.

She doesn't need to be told, she simply rushes over to the door and waits for me to open it. Before I follow her, my eyes catch Sayer's. He's amused as he watches me. Jareth stands close to him and leans in to whisper something. Those two and their rekking secrets. Normally, it doesn't bother me, but when I think they are whispering about my mate, I don't like it.

Ignoring the morts of our faction, I wave my bracelet that grants us access into my chambers. As soon as the doors close behind us, she lets out a gasp.

I relax as I take in my view. My windows remain uncovered. I slathered the glass in sabrevipe blood long ago to keep out the harmful UV rays without obstructing the view. The windows take up the entire far wall and give unobstructed views of the vast wasteland that is our planet.

She walks over to the glass and touches it. When I

come to stand beside her, she looks up at me and gives me what she must think is a brave smile. It's anything but brave, though. My mate is terrified.

"Toto, it doesn't look like we're in Kansas anymore," she whispers.

I fist my hands because the urge to twist my fingers in the messy yellow and brown strands on her nog is becoming too maddening of a thought. "I will keep you safe. From them," I rumble, indicating the other morts. "And from that."

She shivers when my claw plinks on the glass. "We have a deal."

"We have a deal," I agree, understanding her meaning. I try her name on my tongue again. "Molly."

A smile tugs at her lips on one corner, drawing my attention there. "You can call me mate in front of the others if that, you know, helps them understand I'm yours."

Heat wraps around my heart and clenches it tight in a way that actually feels good.

I'm yours.

My mate. My Molly. Mine.

[5]
MOLLY

My hands still tremble, but I hide them in the pockets of my suit, so Draven can't see. For all my bravery so far, it had only taken the thought of hearing the alien baby to bring me back to the shivering thing I'd been when I'd woken up in the cryotube. I'm beyond grateful to Draven for bringing me to his quarters, away from the prying eyes of the others.

I don't even mind the rust-colored blood smeared all over the large windows that cover one wall. It removes some of the light coming in, but it makes the space feel cave-like, cozy. That's not the only thing different about his place.

A nest of pillows and threadbare blankets are piled atop the bedding area, and what look like claw marks mar the walls. Had he done those, or had some sort of wild animal gotten loose? Considering their extreme germaphobia, I'd put money on the former. The marks go almost from ceiling to floor, the ragged edges punctuated by blossoms of dark, red blood.

His rooms remind me of the den of some rabid animal. One who'd attack with the slightest provocation.

Oh, darlin', what happened to you?

I erase those thoughts from my mind. I didn't choose Draven because I wanted to be *closer* to him, I chose him because of all the morts, he's the one who *won't* want to be closer. He's got more walls than a prison, and I have no interest in scaling them.

"Is there a bathroom?" I ask, gesturing down to my clothes. "Do you have somewhere I can get cleaned up?"

He nods toward the wall opposite the windows. "The bathing facilities are through there."

Draven moves when I do, as though he's going to offer to wash me, and I cut him off with a raised arm and a laugh. "Thanks, sugar, but I think I can handle it."

I close the door behind me after a moment of confusion when I merely find buttons on the walls. My shoulders slump, and I press my face into my hands at the first moment of privacy since I stepped out of the cryotube. Tears want to come. I almost wish they would. A good cry would wring me out like an old wash-rag, but they don't come. I'm simply too tired. Too hopeless. I may have limited protection linking myself to Draven, but what happens when I don't immediately get pregnant?

The thought has me stripping out of the suit they provided me as my skin prickles with an uncomfortable heat. The shower is little more than a closet, and it takes me several minutes to figure out the buttons that activate the spray. I step under it and moan in delight as the water cascades over my skin, washing away my fears, if only for a moment.

When I step out, I find clothes waiting for me on a basin. Draven. Touched, I dry off with the thin towel provided and dress in the T-shirt-like apparel. The sleeves have been torn off, and I wonder why as I slip the material over my bare skin. Undergarments must not be one of their priorities.

I find Draven waiting, perched on his nest of blankets, one hand propped on his updrawn knee. A small light buzzes from the ceiling, but it, too, is filmed over with dark, red smears. Whatever had happened to him must have affected his senses. Vision, hearing, touch. The way he held himself separate from the other morts had stood out to me before, but the realization comes back to me now as I watch him watching me.

The others had been so open, friendly. A big family, considering each other is all they have left on this lost planet. But not Draven.

Draven is always apart, other.

An outsider.

And now he's mine.

I cross the room to sit next to him, and he drops his knee, tensing, his hands in loose fists by his sides. The scars on his arms stand out in sharp relief under the dim light.

"What happened to you?" I ask. I consider touching his scars, wondering what caused them, if they still hurt. He always has this look in his eye, like he's in constant pain, tortured.

I don't want to relate to him, to feel the beginnings of affection warming my heart, filling my chest with the soft glow of sympathy, but I do. I, too, know what it feels like to be in pain. To ache with fear.

"The Rades," he grunts, those squinted, black eyes on me.

Tucking my legs up under my body, I angle toward him. Story time before bed always made me sleepy, but I'm too wired to sleep. "Is that like a disease or something?"

He nods. "It took the lives of many morts."

"And that's why there's only ten of you left," I clarify.

"That is correct."

That must have been awful. Probably still is. I guess neither of our lives have exactly been a pile of roses. "How did you survive?"

"If it hadn't been for my commander, I wouldn't have. The disease, it devastated our race. Better morts than me had succumbed to the delirium, the madness. The fever, it's unendurable. Breccan had to lock me in a reform cell to keep me from harming myself or others."

I reach out to take his hand, but he dodges my touch.

At my hurt expression Draven explains, "It's from The Rades. It leaves my skin incredibly sensitive." He fingers the material of my sleep shirt, causing my skin to tingle. "Even the material from my minnasuit irritates my flesh."

I'm only half listening. His fingers are still rubbing the material of my shirt, but his eyes are on my bare skin. Nostrils flaring, his eyes even more shuttered closed than normal, Draven looks crazed, but the heat in his gaze is a look I recognize.

"Well!" I say with false cheerfulness. "I'm beat. I

think it's time to hit the hay. Do you have somewhere I can crash for the night?"

"Crash?" he asks, perplexed. "Are you hurt?"

He looks so perfectly, adorably confused—which should be hard considering how severe he looks most of the time—that I laugh. "No, I mean I'm tired. Do you have a chair or a couch or something I can sleep on?"

"You will share my bed," he answers. "You are my mate. I will protect you."

"I think you can protect me just fine from across the room, big guy."

"I will keep my space. I do not sleep well at night."

Well, that stifles my protests. "Fine," I huff out. "But you stay on your side, and I'll stay on mine."

"As you wish."

He offers me a blanket and tucks me in. It's the first time in recent memory that someone else has taken care of me.

Despite everything that's happened, despite all my fears and worries, I fall into a deep and dreamless sleep with Draven next to me keeping watch.

***

The sound of the baby squalling echoes throughout the facility. My feet carry me from end to end, but I can't escape the sound. Draven is out hunting and glowering at people or else I'd find him to distract me. The other morts are with the commander and his wife. For a bunch of alpha males, they all sure were overjoyed at the opportunity to visit the new bundle of joy.

I begged off with the excuse that I didn't want to intrude, that I needed time to acclimate to my new environment. Sayer and Jareth didn't seem convinced when I told them, but they left me to my own devices to join the others. I'd been fine in Draven's rooms, for a while. Then the baby had started crying, and I could hear it, even behind the closed doors.

Most of the doors I encounter are locked. I assume they're the living quarters of the other aliens and wouldn't offer me any reprieve regardless. I trek all the way across the facility to the sub-faction and back to Draven's before I find a stairwell leading down into darkness. Ordinarily, I wouldn't step blithely into the gloom it offers, but I'm willing to do anything to escape the sounds, the torment.

The darkness lasts for what feels like forever. It's only my probing steps and the vice-like grip I have on the railing that keep me grounded. When I reach the bottom, I search blindly for one of those wall sensors that turn on the lights and manage to find one after a few minutes. The light flicks on with a blinding glow. When my eyes adjust, I gasp.

In front of me are rows of cells on either side of a narrow hallway. I must be in the reform cell place Draven had mentioned. The place where he'd been locked away while he endured the madness caused by The Rades. Without thinking, I walk forward, my head swiveling from side to side as I study the cells and recall my conversation with Draven.

His was the last cell. I know the moment my eyes fall on the destruction inside. Despite the passage of time and the thorough cleaning I imagine it received, shadows of blood still paint the interior. Visions of Draven clawing at his own skin, trying to deafen his own ears, tearing out his own eyes, fill my mind.

Rivets cut into the metal underneath the brown-red stains are twins of those in Draven's room. Based on the extent, I have to wonder if he tried to simply dig his way out of the cell with his own hands. Tortured by delusions, fever, and unimaginable pain, had he tried to escape to end it all? It would be enough to drive anyone to madness.

"You shouldn't be here," comes his voice.

I whirl around and find Draven, his spine straightened to his full, intimidating height, standing at the foot of the stairs. My heart hammers in my throat. I can still hear the baby crying above the sound of blood rushing in my ears. Or am I, too, going mad?

"I'm sorry, I was just..." The baby's screams increase an octave, and I begin to pant. The walls seem to close in around me. I wonder if madness is catching, because clawing my way out of this tin can is starting to seem like a great idea.

"Mate—Molly. What's wrong? Did someone hurt you? Is that why you're hiding?"

The desperation in his voice calms me. "No, I'm fine. I'm just feeling a little...shut in. I wish I could go outside."

Draven studies me, his neck cracking as he reverts back to his normal height. "You wish to see the outside?" he asks.

My thoughts clear. "Can we do that? Go outside. Isn't it dangerous?"

"The winds aren't as violent now that the geostorm is weakening. I will keep you safe, Molly my mate." He lifts a hand for me. "Come with me."

I place my hand in his, comforted by his touch as he is by mine, and follow him back up the stairs, leaving the darkness behind us.

"Where are we going?" I ask when we reach the top. "I thought we weren't allowed."

He tugs me along, passing his quarters, then

Avrell's lab where the doctor had examined me the day before, down a hallway to a door I hadn't yet been through. The tunnel-like walls don't give any hint about where he's leading me, but the volume of the baby's cries begin to decrease and the squeezing sensation around my heart lessens.

Maybe Draven isn't the only one who's a little mad.

He stops when he reaches an outer door and motions for me to wait. He suits up in another of those strange exoskeleton-like suits and fits a mask over his face. Draven does the same for me, extinguishing my hysteria as he carefully helps me into the suit and hooks me into a mask that smells a little strange, but must operate like some sort of breathing apparatus. I don't even care that it makes me feel a little claustrophobic like I did when I was in the cryotube. All I care about is going outside. Being free.

When I'm suited up, he holds a hand out to me.

I take it and he leads me through the doorway and up an endless flight of stairs. I'm shocked at how the urge to follow this broody alien is one that comes easily to me. I'm starting to think I'd follow him anywhere. And that scares the ever-loving fire out of me.

[6]
DRAVEN

Her eyes are wide behind the glass of her mask, and I almost wonder if she is afraid of going to The Tower with me. These alien females seem so fragile and delicate. It's difficult to recall the mort females from long ago. Even when The Rades was destroying them, they were tall and fierce and strong. They were fanged and clawed like the remaining morts. It makes me wonder how these strange aliens manage to exist without proper teeth and claws for defense.

I tap the door and get her attention. "There are dangers outside of this door. You must keep your mask and zu-gear on at all times." I shudder simply thinking about The Rades somehow getting in through a puncture in her suit. Calix has assured me in the past that it's not that simple, but I worry nonetheless. "Also, we must be mindful of armworms."

"Armworms?" she asks, her eyes flicking to the door then back to me.

I show her with my hands how big they are. "They're feral. Sharp teeth. Quick. Territorial. They like to nest up high, away from predators." I unsheathe my magknife. "I will kill them if they try to attack."

Her nog bobs quickly. She clutches my arm over my suit, and for once I don't recoil. The other morts typically don't touch me and respect my...issues. But it's not like it doesn't occasionally happen on accident. Normally, I bolt at such incidents, but with Molly—my mate—I don't feel the pressing need to escape. If anything, I have the urge to reassure her everything will be okay.

"Come, my mate," I grunt.

She gives me a small smile and a nod. I open the door, and she follows behind me. The winds aren't as harsh and unforgiving now that the massive geostorm is finally beginning to move from the area. We won't need harnesses. It makes me wonder if Calix and Emery will travel back to the facility once Emery has given birth to their mortling.

I make quick work of checking The Tower for armworms. There aren't any lurking around, so I guide her over to the northeast side. The mountains in the distance are lit up by the magnastrikes in the geostorm, but just before that, Lake Acido remains visible. The waves are tumultuous on the large, dark, red lake. I scan the parts of the lake that are closest for any beasts roaming. Unfortunately, there are none. I'm growing tired of greenbunches and long for some meat.

"The lake is red," Molly says, pointing. "I thought lakes were supposed to be blue."

I think about the underground wells deep below the facility. Those miniature lakes are bright blue and shimmer in the dark caves. The water is crystal clear, and you can see small sand swimmers on the bottom. When Hadrian was small, he was always getting his rump swatted by Breccan for jumping in after the sand swimmers. Maybe I'll take Molly there one solar soon.

"It's unsuitable for swimming and drinking. The acidic levels are high. Anything that falls into that lake doesn't come out," I tell her. "The beasts don't drink from it but instead find springs that are fed from the underground wells."

"Beasts...like the armworms?"

She scoots closer to me as though she is frightened. I fist my hand. The urge to place my hand on her back and draw her close is nearly maddening. But I would shame myself the moment I lost myself inside my mind. Like when she touched me the moment she hatched from the pod. I'd succumbed to the fear and melted on the spot. It's too risky in The Tower. I need to keep my distance and my mind sorted, so I may keep her protected. I edge slightly away from her.

"Sabrevipes are the most predatory creatures in the vicinity. They're massive, violent, and deadly. Hadrian nearly rekking went to The Eternals from facing off with a young sabrevipe not long ago. They are not to be messed with."

"Lovely," she says, her voice tight. "Are there any animals that are nice? Like farm animals?"

I cock my nog to inspect her. Her lips seem puffier than Aria's and Emery's. Like they are full of something and squishy. If I weren't the way I am, I'd ask her if I could see what her bottom lip felt like under the point of my claw. My curiosity of such silly things has a growl of frustration rumbling from me. This is more Hadrian's area. Curiosity that could get him killed. Something tells me if I go touching this little alien, it'd get me killed, too. I don't know what or why or how, I just get a feeling.

"I do not know these farm animals you speak of."

"Horses? Pigs? Chickens? Cows?"

I slowly nod at her. "We have rogcows. Heavy beasts. Fine tasting meat."

"Do they moo?"

"Moo?"

She lets out a snort of laughter. "Mooooooooo."

My lips twitch. I'm reminded of Hadrian when he was only a few revolutions old running through the facility roaring like a young sabrevipe. He bit Avrell like he was one of those feral beasts. I'd been amused. Our commander, however, was not. Breccan made him wash the entire Facility from top to bottom with a wet cloth, and then he was made to assist Avrell for many solars until he was forgiven. Avrell still has those scars on his forearm.

"They don't moo," I tell her with a smirk. "They ronk."

"Ronk?"

"Ronnnnnnk," I drawl out, my voice growing deeper to mimic the rogcows. "Ronk-ronnnnk."

Her giggles seem to filter through my suit and get inside my veins. The rare smile on my lips fades as I ponder too long on the idea of her laughter being something that's as invasive as The Rades. It's preposterous, but it unnerves me all the same.

"I want to see one," she says, and then she sighs. "I guess I'll never see anything ever again, though. Trapped in this crazy place."

"We are safe here," I assure her. I point to the lake

and the mountains being ravaged by the geostorm. "It's not safe out there." I don't voice that no matter how safe it is in the facility with my faction of morts, I crave to be free. To be out in the harrowing wilderness where I am not contained.

"I like how quiet it is up here," she mutters, her voice barely audible through our comms. "Down there...with them...I couldn't take it."

I frown at her words. "The morts are too noisy for your alien ears?" And here I thought I was the only one who grows agitated over the constant chatter of the other morts.

"Not the guys..." she whispers. "The baby."

Her body is stiff, and she's looking down over the railing. A red, hazy fog hides the rocky bottom below The Tower. The way she stands with her gloved hands gripping the side, it puts me on edge. Like she might suddenly hoist herself over the side. Out of instinct to protect my mate, I gently rest my hand on her lower back.

She snaps her head up to look at me, and her brown eyes are filled with tears. Her bottom lip—the plump, juicy looking one—wobbles wildly. Fire burns inside my chest as the maddening curiosity of what that lip feels like ravages my soul. She captures the moving wonder with her white, blunt teeth and saves me from having to do the job for her.

"What is it that upsets you?" I ask, my voice low and husky.

"Nothing." Her whispered lie has me tensing up. Why does she not speak the truth?

I think back to her remaining in the hallway when I viewed the half-breed born from Aria and Breccan. Did the creature frighten her? It spooked me, but I thought I was the only one.

"The mortling is unusual," I say slowly. "But it is harmless. I viewed it myself." Aside from the claws and fangs, but she doesn't need to know that part.

"It's not harmless." She sniffles and turns toward me. Her heat through her suit nearly scorches me. The urge to push away from her and stalk to the other side of The Tower is strong.

And yet...

I cannot move away from her warmth.

It's always so cold up here. Normally, I don't care. This solar, I don't want to be cold. I want to be warm with my mate.

She moves closer until our fronts are nearly touching. My hand remains at her lower back just above where her rump swells out and stretches the material of her gear. I wonder if she is squishy there like her bottom lip appears to be.

"It is harmless," I assure her.

A tear races down her cheek as she tilts her nog up to look at me. "Draven..."

"Yes, my sweet mate?"

"I did horrible things before ending up here."

"Horrible things?"

"I did what I had to do to protect the one I love."

The one she loves?

Possessiveness surges through my veins, hot and angry. "You have a true mate elsewhere?" I want to spit out the words.

Why do I care?

I'm simply keeping her as a mate to look after her. If she has a true mate on her home planet, I cannot be jealous of such things.

Yet, I am.

"Not a mate," she says, her voice nearly choking on a sob. "A daughter. Willow."

"You have a mortling?"

She nods as more tears stream out. "I...I fought a lot with my baby daddy."

Baby daddy doesn't compute. I don't know what this means.

"Her father," she clarifies, reading the confusion on my face.

"You were the victor?" It must be because she remains standing before me. I knew my mate was strong, unlike Aria and Emery. Pride bursts up inside me.

"He would always hit her…shove her down…kick her…" Her shoulders quake as she sobs. "Willow's just three, Draven. So little. So precious. And Randy was shaking her so bad one day."

My own fears are chased away by the need to comfort my mate. I slide my hand to her rump to grip her and pull her closer. Her rump, through her suit, is every bit as fleshy and full as I'd imagined. I don't want to let her go. I pull her until her front is pressed to mine. Her warmth bleeds into my suit and soothes a cold ache in my bones.

"Did you destroy this Randy?" I growl.

Hadrian was punished often when he was a young mort, but Breccan never hurt him. Simply swatted his bottom as a reminder. Never out of anger. Not like this monster named Randy.

"I did," she chokes. "I was so afraid of Randy. He would hit me, too, even after we divorced, but I'm stronger. I could take it."

I snarl, my grip on her rump tightening as though I can protect her from the monster in her past.

"We were in the kitchen when he came to pick her up for a visitation. All...all I could hear was Willow crying for me to help her. I couldn't take it. I saw red, Draven." Her eyes flash with fierce protectiveness. "I stabbed him."

"This Randy deserved to have his skin flayed from his bones," I hiss out. "Males do not strike females or mortlings. That is insanity." Even maddened by The Rades, I would've never hurt someone weaker than me. Randy is like Aria's monster, Kevin. And we morts are *not* Kevins.

"It was meant to stop him temporarily," she mutters. "How was I supposed to know I'd nick a main artery in his neck? All I wanted was to get him off my baby girl." Her eyes grow distant. "There was so much blood. But Willow was safe. That's all that mattered." She bows her head in shame. "They took my daughter after that. I was sentenced to life on Exilium. He died, Draven. I killed him. A man I once loved enough to have a baby with."

Since we are safe from armworms, I sheathe my magknife and slide my other hand to her rump. It feels right to hold her here. With our suits on, touching her is easy.

"You were brave, my mate."

She shakes her nog. "Brave? It was the ultimate sin. Murder. They took my daughter and sent me away. I am never going to see her again. My future was to remain in a cell like the ones you guys have until the day I died."

"Your planet sickens me," I snarl. "They punish those who protect the weak?"

"I'd do it all over again if it meant saving my daughter from that monster's abusive hand," she tells me in a fierce tone. "Hearing that baby crying just makes me think about my sweet Willow and it hurts, Draven. It just hurts." She lets out a ragged sigh that rasps through the comms system. "I bet you guys wish you wouldn't have intercepted that ship now, huh? Took a bunch of bad girls and saved them from doing life in prison. What did the other two do?"

"Aria remembers nothing about the ship. I'm not sure Emery does either."

"Unfortunately, I remember everything."

I give her rump a comforting squeeze that feels right in this moment. "We must tell the others. The commander will want to know this information."

"I'm sorry," she utters. "If you want to put me in one of your cells, I'll understand."

Shaking my nog, I find her sad stare. "You're my

mate, and I will not allow anyone to lock you away in a reform cell. This is my promise to you."

"Thank you," she breathes. Her arms wrap around my middle, and she rests her head against my chest. I'm tense at the affectionate gesture, but I don't push her away.

No, I give her rump another two-handed squeeze.

This feels right.

This feels right.

This feels rekking right.

[7]
MOLLY

"Will you stay with me? I don't want to be alone, and this is hard enough as it is."

Draven's hands still as he helps me out of the over-suit—or zu-gear as he refers to it—and mask that I've learned is called a rebreather after a rigorous, decontaminating cleansing. "Of course, my mate. I won't be going anywhere." He sheds his own suit and stores our gear, before turning to me. "We must speak with Breccan and Aria at once. Any information you may know about you and the other aliens is vital."

I nod and barely notice as he tugs me back to the corridor where Breccan and his mate, Aria, are resting with their newborn. Well, I barely notice anything other than the warmth of Draven's hand clasped securely around my own. When I told him about what

I'd done, the kind of person I am, he'd looked at me like...he was proud of me. No one has ever been proud of me before. No one has ever looked at me like he did.

No one has ever made me feel safe.

Draven may be big and scary and probably crazy, but he is mine now.

Before I know it, we're at the door. Draven waits for an announcement to come in, then swipes his card, and the door slides open. I hesitate in the doorway until Draven turns with a curious look and tugs me forward. This time, I go inside and meet the authoritative commander once more, under better terms, and finally his human wife, Aria.

Breccan hovers over Aria, who is curled up in their bed. He turns when he sees us. "You said over the comms that you had news about the females. Come in."

The baby squalls and Aria soothes him with a low hum. My throat turns to dust, and my knees lock. Draven glances back curiously, notes my distress, and comes immediately to my side. I could get used to having him around.

"Yes, Commander," Draven answers as he positions himself behind me, almost wrapped around me. My protector. "I was speaking with my mate, and she shared with me that she remembers her past, where she came from. With the other two aliens having no memory of how they came to be on the ship, I thought it wise to come to you with this news immediately."

Aria, who'd been thoroughly distracted by the slumbering bundle in her arms, springs to attention at his words. "She what?"

"The female told you about this?" Breccan demands.

I press my back into Draven's chest, but when I speak, I keep my voice even. "You can talk to me. I'm right here. Besides, I'm the one with the answers you want. Yes, I told him. And I'll tell you what I can."

Snap.

Draven's neck starts cracking behind me, and I grip his hand to calm him.

Sensing the tension between the two males, Aria mirrors my movement and places a soothing hand on Breccan's arm. I guess this is what humans and mort males have in common; if it weren't for women, no one would ever get anything done.

"We should get Sayer to call Emery and Calix on the comms," Aria suggests. "She may have questions or be able to fill in any blanks that Molly can't."

"Draven," Breccan directs.

I squeeze his hand to let him know it's okay, and he leaves me with the other two to go summon Sayer.

An ache settles over my chest as I watch Breccan become distracted by the cooing little form in Aria's arms. The two of them huddle over their baby with identical smiles of contentment, smiles I recognize. I'd felt like that once. Once upon a time, the woman smiling at the baby had been me.

Aria notices me staring and lifts the baby in my direction. "Would you like to hold him?"

I clear my throat. Tears prickle. "No, thank you." I soften my words with a smile, and begin to hum under my breath, wondering how long it'll take Draven to return. It's not a good sign that I can only go a few minutes without his presence before I feel like I'm coming apart at the seams. "La la, la la, la," I hum.

"Are you sure? I don't mind," Aria insists.

I hum louder, pretending I don't hear her. "LA LA, LA LA LAAAA."

The two of them share looks, but I pretend I don't notice. An eternity passes until the doors reopen and Draven strides through with Sayer, the one with the long hair. This time it's flowing all the way down to his butt. He's carrying a device that he immediately sets up at Aria's bedside, pausing to coo at the bundle in Aria's arms.

"Emery," Sayer says into the device. "Calix, this is Sayer."

A crackle fills the line. Sayer repeats himself several times before another voice fills the room. "This is Calix, receiving transmission. Is everything all right?"

Sayer nods to Breccan, who says, "We've good news, my friend. Aria delivered our mortyoung. We named him for my father, Sokko."

"That is great news, Commander. Emery will have a thousand questions, and me as well. Did—"

"I'll have Avrell update you with the details. I'm afraid we're calling for a different reason. Another female has woken."

"Oh?" Calix replies.

"She remembers where the ship came from, where it was headed. We thought Emery should be present for the conversation. Is she with you?"

"I'm here, Breccan. Aria, congratulations on your baby. We're so happy for you."

"Thank you," Aria says, still glowing. "Emery, I'd like to introduce you to Molly. A magnastrike caused her cryotube to malfunction. She woke up during a lot of the confusion not too long ago, so we haven't had time to properly introduce her to everyone."

"When do we ever have time to do anything properly?" Emery asks dryly. "Pleased to meet you, Molly. My mate, Calix, and I are at Sector 1779 across the mountains. I woke up several months ago, and we had to travel here to use their medical facilities. I'm looking forward to hearing from you and filling in the holes in my memory."

"Why don't you start with the shuttle?" Aria suggests when I don't answer. The baby in her arms has quieted and so have my thoughts.

My tongue unsticks itself from the roof of my mouth. I sense Draven behind me, and my chest unclenches. "What would you like to know?"

"Anything you remember. I'm afraid my memory is a complete blank, so any information you have would be helpful."

There's a loud *scrape* of metal against floor as Draven drags a chair over, urging me to sit on his lap. The other morts watch us with keen fascination, but my thoughts are too jumbled to work out why. "Well, first, I suppose I should tell you that I'm not a perfect person. I've made mistakes in my past. I was on the shuttle because I killed my ex-husband, who was abusive. He used to beat me and my child, and I couldn't take it anymore." I say the last bit quickly, trying to gloss over the bit about Willow as fast as possible so the image of her sweet face doesn't materialize, but it's no use. Speaking of her so much, knowing I may never see her again, has the pain of her loss rolling over me in great waves. I hum a little, losing the thread of conversation, and Draven nuzzles his cheek against my arm.

"You say you were on the shuttle because you killed your ex-husband?" Emery prompts. Was it a trick of the static from the comms unit, or did she sound a little breathless?

I nod, even though she can't see me. "Yes. I was sentenced to life on Exilium for my crime." The next part is so hard to say, I nearly choke. "My daughter was taken to live with another family, and I was being transported on the shuttle to carry out my sentence."

"Kevins," Breccan growls inexplicably. "Your alien males are all *Kevins*."

I don't understand what he means by that, but Draven seems to because he nods in agreement, his cheek brushing against my arm again. Aria whispers to Breccan, and he settles.

"The same is true for my Emery," Calix says over the comms unit. "She was also sentenced to life imprisonment."

Breccan's eyebrows lift in surprise, and Draven stiffens at this information which appears to be new to them.

"I suppose I shouldn't be shocked at this development," Breccan says, turning to his mate, pride evident on his fearsome face. "I have no doubt you must have been en route to Exilium as well, Aria. My mate is a fighter."

Aria shakes her head in disbelief. "No, I couldn't have been...could I?" She turns to me with a quizzical look.

The change of topic helps revitalize me, and I breathe deeply for the first time since Draven led me back inside. "I'm sorry to be the one to tell you, but you were on the shuttle as well." A blush stains my cheeks. "I only know this because I recognized you, you know from the movies. You're a pretty famous actress back home."

"Do you remember what I was there for?" Aria asks. "Surely it was a mistake."

"Well," I murmur, "it was all over the news..."

If she doesn't remember, then I don't know if I want to be the one to tell her.

"Go on," Breccan urges.

"You, uh..." I start, skimming my gaze to Draven who nods for me to continue. "You set your talent manager's home on fire." I flash her a sympathetic look. "With him in it."

"Kevin?" she chokes out, her eyes going wide.

Breccan and Draven both growl.

"Yeah, him," I say softly. "Everyone said it was

because you were high, but by the way you were screaming obscenities on live television at the burning home and how you hoped he rots in hell, it had me drawing my own conclusions."

I know all about horrible men. And her crime, like mine, was one of passionate fury.

"I killed Kevin," she whispers, her voice trembling. "Holy shit. I killed Kevin."

Breccan grins proudly at her. "Rekking right you did!"

Draven grunts his approval and nods at her.

Breccan starts to say something else, but she slaps a hand over his mouth before he can speak and balances the baby on one arm. "Don't you say a word," she warns before speaking to Emery on the comms. "You didn't know this?"

"Bits and pieces have come back to me since the surgery. I knew about the penitentiary at Exilium, but I didn't know where or who you were back where we're from," she answers, then adds, "To be honest, I was afraid to admit what little I knew until I confessed everything to Calix."

"Do you know where the reformation camp was located?" Sayer asks with his pen poised above a notebook. "Exilium you say? Never heard of it."

I shake my head. "Everything's a little blurry. It

happened so fast." I begin to hum again and turn away from them. Too much. It's too much.

Draven, who'd been quiet as we spoke, takes over. "We'll speak to Theron about accessing the flight plans and data from their shuttle. Perhaps if we can identify a destination, we'll learn more."

The baby begins to cry, and I shoot to my feet. Draven stands and murmurs something in my ear I don't understand, but his voice is soothing, already familiar. Avrell is called for, and he rushes in to join the meeting, his worried gaze only for Aria and her child. I've said all I've come to say, so I fall silent.

"We must go, Breccan," Calix says. "Be well."

Sayer slips out as Avrell begins to examine the squalling infant. I swear I see fangs, but I could be mistaken. It's been a long day.

"Is he eating well?" Avrell asks as he takes measurements and readings.

Aria smiles sweetly, exhausted. I want to tell her I remember the feeling, but the words won't come. "Almost around the clock," she says. "Avrell, be straight with me. It's only been a short while, but I can tell something is wrong. He doesn't seem settled. He eats a lot, and I know I could be the fretful first-time mom, but I've got a gut instinct that's telling me he isn't getting enough."

Avrell sighs, rubbing his eyes. "We've learned that mortyoung grow at an accelerated rate compared to humans. He was born earlier than typical human young, yet much larger despite the reduced gestation. But, uncharacteristic to normal mortyoung, he rapidly shed his birthweight at an exceedingly alarming rate. I thought maybe it would take time for his vitals to even out, but they're not showing as much improvement as I'd like. And though it is normal for mortyoung to lose a certain percentage of weight after birth, little Sokko is losing too much, too fast. So, I'm sorry Aria, Commander, but yes, I think you're right. He isn't getting enough nutrients from your milk alone."

A tear falls down Aria's cheek, the earlier revelations already forgotten. "What can we do?"

"When my little one wasn't getting enough from me alone, I had to supplement with formula," I say. I don't know where the words come from, because that certainly couldn't have been my voice. No. I turn away, but they're already taking my contribution and running with it.

Avrell perks up. "You remember when Hadrian was but a few micro-revolutions, when we had to give him so much rogcow milk, we thought he'd drink the whole herd dry? We could perhaps do the same for young Sokko. With the combination of mort and alien genes, it could be that the mortyoung will need more nutrients. It's worth the risk to travel," Avrell says.

As the others speak, I let Draven lead me away from the sound of their voices until the doors slide shut behind us.

"It's all right, my Molly. I've got you. Let me take you back to our quarters. I'll have Galen fetch some of those goldenroot candies you aliens like so much. You can rest, and I'll bring you to eat once Breccan has finished speaking with Avrell."

"I don't want to talk about that anymore. At least not now. I know there are things you need to know—it just hurts." I stop him before we enter his quarters, meeting his eyes. "Please?"

Draven brushes the hair away from my face. "I understand pain, my Molly. And I'll do whatever I can to take yours away."

[8]
DRAVEN

TWO SOLARS.

All it took was two solars to go from peace to rekking madness. Every single mort and the two females here are on edge.

It's the mortling, Sokko.

I've never heard anything screech so loudly and for so long.

Never rekking ending.

Avrell has been working tirelessly to extract more milk from Aria's breasts in an effort to duplicate its properties while Galen scans our region for rogcow herds. The geostorm is out of the way now, but The Graveyard is barren and empty of life, which is typical after these climatic events. All Galen needs to do is give me word on where a herd is, and I'll hunt down those rekking rogcows.

"You're pacing," Molly says from our bed.

I pull away from my inner turmoil to regard her. This solar she is irresistible. I'm finding it more and more difficult to keep my hands from her. All I want is to take hold of her fleshy rump and squeeze it. At night, when she slumbers, her face burrows against my chest, and I take my fill of her bottom in my hands. She never pushes me away. It's as though the touch comforts her, too.

"We need to find a herd," I say absently, stalking over to the bed to sit beside her.

She's perched on her knees, and when I relax beside her, she wraps her slender arms around me. Hugging. She calls these squeezes of energy hugs. I asked Avrell if the aliens have special abilities because my mate seems to send bursts of life thrumming through my veins during these episodes. He told me it's a four-letter word I don't know yet. I suspect he was having amusement at my expense and have been agitated ever since.

I nuzzle my face against the side of her neck that smells sweet and mouth-watering. Her scent is one I've grown quite addicted to. She has claws, too, but they are different. Rounded and thinner. The same color as her flesh. And her claws are not useless as I once thought. They contain their own abilities.

To calm.

The moment she rakes her claws through the patchy hair on my nog, it has a relaxing effect on my body. I would ask Avrell, but I do not choose to be laughed at again. One of my arms wraps around her middle, and I try to mimic her hugs. I don't have the same powers as her, but I try to show through my actions that I wish I did. She seems to appreciate my attempts because she rewards me with her lovely signing as she calls it and her calm clawing.

"Do you think they'll ever find the herds?" she murmurs, her hot breath tickling the top of my nog.

My lips whisper over her flesh. "Not any time soon. The geostorms have sent them into hiding. Places where the scanners aren't picking up."

She shivers. "Do you think Sokko will die?"

I wince at that thought. Though the mortling is unappealing to look at, I don't want it to die. Breccan and Aria—everyone besides Molly and myself—look at the miniature beast as though it is wrought from the sun itself. Bright and beautiful. It would break this faction if we lost our first true hope for a future on our planet. The Eternals are no place for a mortling. Breccan might retreat to his dark, inner thoughts for good this time. This is something I cannot allow. He brought me from my darkness, and I refuse to let him go there. The darkness is a place no mort should ever go.

"I need to hunt them," I utter, mostly to myself.

Molly pulls away and ceases her clawing, much to my dismay. "You want to go out there and look for them anyway?"

"It is necessary," I tell her in a solemn tone.

Her brown eyes sheen with unshed tears. "I'll come with you."

"No," I growl so fiercely she jumps. "It is unsafe."

She gapes at me. "If it's so unsafe, then why are you going?"

"Because someone must do it, and I am the only one with the skills to do so."

"I'm coming with you," she snips. "When? Tonight?"

When she starts to move off the bed, I grip her wrists, pulling her close enough that our noses touch. "You're staying here, my mate."

She scoffs. "Absolutely not. I have skills, too. I grew up on a freakin' farm, Draven. I know all about hunting and animals. I'm going."

"No," I snarl, panic rising up inside me. My lips brush against hers. They are softer and plumper than I imagined. I want to investigate them further. If only I had more time. "I beg of you."

She puckers her lips and presses them to mine. It's like a hug for our lips. The energy she emits zaps through my veins, invigorating my every cell. Her hands break free of my hold as they slide into my hair once more. I let out a groan of appreciation. The moment my lips part as the sound escapes, my mate surprises me.

Sweet.

Maddening.

Delicious.

Her taste slides across my forked tongue, stealing my every thought that isn't her. My tongue lashes at hers, desperate for more of her unique flavor. I can't help but grab her hips to pull her closer to me. Her legs settle on either side of me, and her center presses against my cock that is achingly hard, straining against my minnasuit.

"Draven," she moans, her hips rocking like they sometimes do when she sings.

I hiss and grab her round rump with more force than I intended. She cries out and nips my bottom lip.

Fire burns through my entire body as I lose my mind to the sensations she is flooding me with.

Her fingers tug at my hair, and she pulls my nog back. Brown eyes blaze with a hunger I've never seen on anyone before. It's as though she wants to consume me. I try to recall what I know about mating. It was something I didn't read for myself, but overheard Breccan speaking of not long after he started mating with Aria.

Remove the clothes.

Lick her cunt until she cries.

Make her wet with arousal, so she can take your cock.

Breccan didn't say what happened next, but Hadrian demonstrated against the wall, making terrible noises as he pretended to rut.

I think I can figure it out.

"My mate," I mutter, squeezing her rump. "Would you ever...would you consider..."

Taking my cock?

The words die on my tongue.

Shame creeps up along my flesh, making it burn hot.

"W-What?" she stammers. "What is it that you want from me?"

Her heated stare sears into me.

"I want to put my cock—"

Bang! Bang! Bang!

We're jolted from the moment as someone interrupts us. She slides off my thighs with a surprised shriek. I'm already storming toward the door in the next moment.

"What is it?" I demand as I swipe my access card.

The door slides open, and Avrell storms in. His hair is messy, and his tired eyes are wild.

"I can't do it, Draven. I can't mimic the milk properties, even with Calix's help on the comms. Not even Galen can figure it out." He lets out a heavy sigh. "How am I to tell Breccan that his mortling will go to The Eternals because I cannot find a solution?"

Molly bounds up from the bed, rushing over to us. She loops her arm with mine and reaches out to touch Avrell's shoulder with her other hand.

"Babycakes," she coos. "We've got this."

I look down at her, my brow lifted in question. She simply lifts her chin and does a one-eyed blink. Is her other eyelid broken?

"My mate and I," she says breathlessly, "are going to hunt for a herd. How soon can we travel?"

Relief floods through Avrell at her words, and he gives me a hopeful smile. "Truly? You're to hunt down a herd?"

I cock my nog at him, confused. Avrell is all for the protection of the females, yet here he is, willing to let my mate go out into The Graveyard to assist me in my hunt. This has me realizing the importance of this task. What is the point of impregnating the females if their young will be sent to The Eternals within days? I would never do such a horrible thing to my Molly. She's already grieved over the loss of one life.

"My mate farmed," I tell Avrell, confidence in my tone. I flick my gaze at Molly to make sure I said the right term. She nods her nog as she smiles. I continue, "She farmed and knows of hunts on her planet. There are beasts here similar to what she is familiar with. She is skilled with a magknife and will kill when necessary as she proved with her Kevined Randy. My mate is a valuable asset to this mission."

And I am selfish.

I want her by my side.

I will protect her from any beast out there. Any storm. Anything.

"We must make haste then," Avrell growls, motioning for us to follow. I've never seen him so maddened. Calix, yes. Breccan, most definitely. Never Avrell. With the arrival of our aliens, it's as though we're all performing at elevated levels of protection and determination. We care for them, and they are vital to our success of continuity on this planet.

As soon as we make it into the corridor, the screams of the mortling echo louder than before.

Avrell stops and turns abruptly. Sadness flashes in his dark eyes. "He's losing too much weight. Another five, maybe six solars, and..." His brows furl together. "I need you back, a ronking rogcow in tow, within four. We cannot take any chances, Draven. Sokko's tender life depends on it."

Molly and I both nod our nogs.

Time is of the utmost importance.

***

As we gather supplies, my eyes drift to Sayer. He has Molly pulled close as he speaks to her. She doesn't seem to be in duress, so I allow his proximity for now. When Jareth pops in between them, slinging both of his arms across each of their shoulders, the only thing that stops me from ripping him away from her is her loud chuckle.

She is not frightened.

Galen hands me a pouch, drawing my attention away from the other morts and my mate. "This is dried chaxen. You will need it."

I open the pouch and peer at the green dust. "What is it?"

"It's derived from mosshay I grow in my lab. It's something rogcows eat. Where it can be found, the rogcows are plentiful. Sometimes it grows in patches near Lake Acido after a drenching geostorm. When the mosshay is dried out and crushed, it becomes this dust." He tugs at the pouch strings to close it. "Sprinkle it around your camp at night. Leave a trail of it from the facility to wherever you go. If the winds are just right, the rogcows can smell it from farther than the eye can see. They will come."

"Are you sure?" I ask.

He frowns for a moment, uncertainty glimmering in his black eyes. Then, he lifts his chin. "It has to work, Lieutenant. It absolutely must."

He stows the pouch in a large bag. We have to go on foot, so everything must be carried on our backs.

"Here," Oz says, striding around the corner with a small zuta-metal box in his hand. "It's the best I could do on such short notice. A vacuu-pod. Smaller than the vacuu-room I made for Calix and Emery. The entire unit has decontamination properties. You'll notice there's a sheen of white powder once you open the pod. It's a cleansing agent that sucks and eliminates harmful toxins both in the air and on surfaces. I apologize that it's small, but it will do the job." He flashes me a wide grin, showing off his double fangs.

"Might have to hold the mate close. Not much room in there."

I let out a warning growl because I don't like the way his eyes travel over her. He tosses me the vacuu-pod box and bounces down the corridor before I can give him a good knock to his nog. I shove the box into my pack and rise to my feet.

Breccan enters the corridor where we're all standing, his features haggard and weary. He stalks over to me, standing too close for my comfort. "Thank you, my friend," he rasps out. "This journey is important."

"We're gonna wrangle you a cow," Molly assures him, coming to stand beside me. Her hand threads with mine. "Isn't that right, mate?"

I don't correct her to tell her that it's called a rogcow. It warms me how sure of our success she is.

"If they exist, I will find them," I growl in response.

The mortling's screams echo louder than before, causing Breccan to shudder. Despair is reflected on his features, and it makes me want to bring him all the rekking rogcows on this planet.

"You'll leave at first light," he grunts out. "It's too late to set out on the journey. Rest your nogs for now."

I finish packing up while Molly interrogates the remaining morts in the corridor. She's asking about the terrain, the weather, and creatures we may encounter.

Pride surges through me. She is my mate. I have never had a partner to assist me on a mission. Typically, I do solo missions if possible. When the other morts come with, they do one thing, while I do another. Sometimes, Breccan injects himself to aid me, but I never need his assistance.

I don't need Molly's assistance either.

But I want her company.

She bends to push something into her bag and puts her juicy round rump on display for me. My cock thickens in my minnasuit. The urge to rut against her becomes a maddening roar inside my nog.

When she lifts and turns to regard me, I can't hide my need for her. Her brown eyes are soft, but as they drag down the front of my minnasuit where my cock strains, they grow fiery hot. She bites on her bottom lip. It makes me want to take a bite, too.

"Time for bed," she announces, her voice breathy.

I sniff the air, catching the smallest hint of her female scent.

And like a mort on a hunt, I stalk after my prey.

The only difference is, she doesn't run or hide.

No, my mate runs right into my arms.

I grab her round rump in both hands as she wraps her legs around my waist. My claws puncture the minnasuit she's wearing, and she whimpers when the sharp points tease along her bare flesh beneath.

Ignoring the open mouths of Sayer and Jareth, and the flare of envy in Galen's eyes, I storm off with my mate.

It's time to make her mine in every sense of the word.

[9]
MOLLY

I LET HIM CARRY ME, mindless of the others, until we reach the hall. Then, with a flirty, fiery look over my shoulder, I dart off for his quarters with him close on my heel. He gives chase with a growl that sends shock-waves along my skin.

Tomorrow, we'll hunt, but tonight, I'm the prey, and he is the predator.

I make it all the way to his door where I'm stymied by the lack of an armband to unlock the door. But it doesn't matter because he's there, pinning me against the cool metal, before I have a moment to consider my next move. His towering form blots out any light, and in the shadows cast by his body, it feels like we're the only two left on this lonely, lost planet.

"Shouldn't we, I don't know, get ready for the hunt

tomorrow?" My words are as useless as my lungs, which struggle to find air. There's nothing we can do while it's dark out, but my mouth moves without conscious decision.

His dark, crazed eyes roam over me hungrily as though he can see through the material of my suit. I itch to have his gaze replaced by his hands. "There'll be no work tonight, unless you count what I want to do to you as work." He cocks his head to the side as though amused. If I wasn't mistaken, he almost looks like he's...smiling. Draven smiling?

He waves an arm at the sensor by the door, and it glides open, the emptiness beckoning us inside. Draven takes one step forward, our bodies brushing, and I take a step back. He does this again and again until we're in the solitude of his rooms. Once the doors close, we're completely alone with only the double moon glow from the other side of the blood-smeared window to illuminate the cave-like space.

"Are you sure we should do...this?" I babble. "I mean, this was only supposed to be something platonic. We were going to be each other's safe space, you know? If we bump uglies and it goes bad, we're going to be stuck in this place with each other. If it goes bad, it'll go really bad."

Finally, my back reaches the far wall, and there's nowhere else to go.

"There is no part of you that is ugly, Molly mate. Every part of you is beautiful." His claws scratch against my minnasuit. "I will investigate further to prove it to you this solar."

He moves to unzip my suit, and I stop him with a hand. "Whoa there, buckaroo. Even though I don't think it's a good idea, if we're going to do this, we need to take it slow."

"Take it slow?" he asks. "I can do this."

I gulp. The closer he gets to me, the faster I want to go. It's been so long since I've let loose that the heat is washing away all my common sense. *Keep it together, Molly girl.* I open my mouth to explain, but Draven covers it with his.

So much for the rest of my common sense.

This is all so new between us, but already, kissing him feels a little bit like being at home. I've never had a place I truly called home, not really, but if I did, it would be in Draven's arms.

I taste a bit of the madness inside him in the kiss. Tangy and wild. His kiss is unfettered, a temptation. The rabbit leading me down the bottomless whole. I should be cautious. Should try to keep my head on straight to figure out my next move, but then he shifts, the kiss deepens, and I leap without thinking.

Before, he hadn't known what to do with his mouth, his tongue, but a few short kisses and it's as though he's soaked up all the knowledge of seduction the universe has to offer. He parries my defenses with hard, dominating kisses that leave my lips tender and bruised, then soft, drugging kisses where he drags my bottom lip in, sucking it, then nipping it with his teeth and releasing.

My hands can't seem to find a good place to hold onto him, so they travel all over the shorn shoulders of his suit, to the scarred expanse of his thickly muscled arms. I scratch my fingernails through his hair in the way that makes him moan into my mouth. Then his lips are breaking free and licking down my throat.

"Your taste, it's better than the sweetest sparkle-berry fruit," he whispers against my skin. His touch is surprisingly gentle and sweet, his claws retracting so his fingertips trace over every visible inch, leaving a swath of goose bumps in their wake.

I've lost the ability to speak. He's stolen it from me with each passing, fire-bright touch, each lost second. When he reaches the hem of my top at the neckline, he pulls away, but presses a hand on my belly to keep me still. I may not be able to speak, but his message is crystal clear. I'm not to move from this spot. My knees are locked, and even if they weren't, I'm not sure there's anywhere else I'd rather be.

As I'm held in position, he strips himself out of the top of his suit, revealing acres of gorgeous, muscled chest, powerful shoulders, and an abdomen that ripples as he flexes. Saliva floods my mouth, and I shiver from simply looking at him. He is mine as much as I'm his.

Maddeningly, he stops with the bottom of his suit hanging limply from his hips. An intriguing bulge tents the front, and nothing has ever tempted me so much. I could ignore his directive to stay pinned to the wall as he torments me, half afraid of what he'll do if I move and half intrigued by what he'll do next.

He extends his claws long enough to rip into my shirt, easily shredding the material until it falls to a limp pile at my feet. My breasts, which I'd bound with extra material, spring free, and I hiss as the cool air turns my nipples into hard nubs. His eyes drink in my half-naked form greedily, and as though he can't resist, his mouth comes to one breast, laving the sensitive tip with the forked end of his tongue.

I throw my head back, cupping his neck with my hands, holding him to my chest. When I begin tugging at his hair, he switches to my other breast, nuzzling and nipping until I cry out.

"I like hearing you call out for me. Before the next solar, I want to hear you call out until you no longer have a voice."

"Draven, please."

"Please, what?" he teases.

"More. Touch me more."

"Where do you want me to touch you, Molly mate?"

I shove at my pants. "Take these off. Touch me where it aches. Let me touch you. Anything. Please."

"We have all night until the hunt. I wish we had more time. I'd mate with you for solars and solars."

I nearly sob in desperation. "We don't have solars. We've got tonight, and I want you so bad it hurts."

He kisses me again, and I've never felt anything as good as his bare chest against mine. The sensation drives me wild, and I forget my resolve to stand still, to be patient like he requested. Instead, I launch myself at him, my legs tangling in the half-on, half-off status of my pants. Confined the way I am, I can't get close enough to press that bulge against the heat between my thighs where I want it most.

Draven twists and angles his body, so he has us both on his pallet of blankets. With infinite patience, he settles me against his side, freeing my restless feet and legs of my shoes, then the rest of my suit, until I'm naked next to him. At the sight of my bared body he stills, his hand hovering over me.

"What are you doing?" I ask as the seconds lengthen with him only gazing at me.

"Looking at you. I want to remember you like this always. My mate is so beautiful it makes me forget the madness."

Touched beyond words, I pull him down against me, a little dismayed to find he's still only halfway out of his suit. Then, he starts where he left off, kissing me down my chest in a determined path to the valley of my thighs.

I throw my head back against his blankets as he fits himself between my legs, his wide shoulders spreading me open for his gaze and then, for his mouth. I'd thought feeling his tongue on my nipples was devastating.

I'd been wrong.

His forked tongue scissors the sensitive nub of my clit, stroking and licking until it's so sensitive I can feel my heartbeat throbbing wildly against his flesh. Sheathed fingertips probe the slick opening of my cunt, and I sob unintelligible words until he thrusts inside. His shoulders nudge me wider, his finger pressing so deep inside it's almost painful. When he bottoms out, the fleshy part of his palm presses against my clit, sending sharp zings of pleasure along my nerve endings.

"I like your sweetness on my tongue." He licks his fingers for emphasis, then pushes two inside. "Wider," he says, nudging my legs apart.

I moan and grip his shoulders because that's all I can do. Hold on.

His fingers are thick and meaty, as strong as the mort himself, using only the amount of restraint he thinks I require, his fingers pounding into me. He works with a singlemindedness that's infectious. There is only the deep thrust, then slow drag until the pads of his fingers brush against the front walls of my cunt, dragging the first feral scream from my throat as I'm suspended on the precipice of an orgasm. He fixes his tongue on my clit, sucking the throbbing bundle into his mouth as he repeats the thrust and drag. It's the combination of the two that has me succumbing to a pleasure so acute it's almost violent.

When my eyes refocus, I find him dragging his pants down and off, flinging them over his shoulder and beyond. He crawls up my replete body, a satisfied gleam in his eyes. This alien likes that he knows how to please me. Likes it so much he wants more.

And I want nothing more than to give it to him.

Give him everything.

I take him into my arms, relishing in the feel of his weight on top of me, my cunt aching to be filled. I draw him close with one leg and meet his kiss, tasting myself on his wicked, wicked tongue. For someone who doesn't talk much, he sure knows how to use it.

"I like the way you scream," he says against my mouth.

But I have no time for words. The brush of pleasure has ignited something more inside me. A fire without end. I grip his shoulders and wrap my other leg around his strong hips. The bulbous head of his cock slicks through my folds, ripping a gasp from my dry throat.

"My mate wants my cock."

I nod, but I don't know if he sees me. Nothing seems to make sense. There's only the urge for completion, fulfillment. I strain to fit him inside me, but he evades me.

I open my eyes and glare at him.

He smiles, a true smile tinged with the same wildness I feel coursing through me. If I weren't so needy and desperate, I would have been overjoyed.

"Don't smile at me, Draven. Yes, I want your cock. Please."

"This is what I want to hear."

He surges forward, filling me so completely, my retort is forgotten as my brain stutters to a stop. It should be impossible for something to feel better than his fingers and tongue working in tandem, but his cock filling me, thrusting deep and hard, is a pleasure that's immeasurable.

Wanting to make him lose control, to see that wildness overtake him, has me gripping him tight against me. I pull him down until I can kiss him again, taste our combined flavors and get drunk off them. I give him everything I have, sucking, licking deep, and exploring the strong expanse of his back and chest with my hands. I knead and scratch at his sweat-glossed skin, accepting each of his sounds of pleasure with my mouth.

His thrusts snap harder but are still tempered by control, still tamed. For someone who always seems to be controlling himself, getting him let loose is near impossible. I throw everything into seducing him toward the edge. I kiss him with wild abandon, spreading my legs in explicit invitation, causing him to groan.

"I want you. I want all of you like you have me."

The corded muscles in his throat stand out in relief. When he speaks, his voice vibrates with the effort to control himself. "When you take my pleasure, Molly mate, you will be unable to move for some time. I won't hurt you."

I soften beneath him, wrapping him fully in my arms. "Is that what you're worried about? I know you won't hurt me. I trust you." I'm not sure what he means by not being able to move, but I know he'll be there for me, whatever happens.

It's as though my words unlock something inside of him. He rears back and grips the backs of my thighs in his hands, pinning my lower body to the bed by the force of his grip. His thrusts are powerful and all-consuming. Sweat beads at his forehead and rolls down his cheeks as he chases his own pleasure.

"You first," he grunts.

He says something, but I don't know what it is. Seeing him lose it is more intoxicating than the strongest orgasm. Mine roars up from the ether and consumes me. All I can focus on is the swell of the wave, building, threatening to crest and take me under.

I grapple underneath me for something to hold onto, something to ground me because I know when it happens, it's going to obliterate everything.

"Molly," he grunts and says something else, but it's blotted out as I clench around his still furiously pumping cock.

Pleasure bursts out of me, compounds, then explodes again, overtaking my body with tremors.

At the sound of my orgasm, Draven shouts, rocking his hips into me several times before his body goes impossibly taut. Heat spurts inside of me, and there's a moment of pure silence and peace before I realize what he meant about not being able to move.

"Shh," he whispers as he pulls out of me to gather me close in his arms. Even though he still shudders in the aftershocks from his own orgasm, he's solely focused on comforting me as my panicked gaze meets his. "Don't worry, I won't let anything happen to you. The paralyzing effect of the toxica will wear off shortly."

There's something to be said for basking in the moment after sharing intimacy. As the paralytic takes effect, I have no choice but to allow him to pet and soothe. His claws rake over my sensitized skin, and it's almost as pleasurable as the act of sex itself.

By the time I'm able to move again, there isn't anywhere else I'd rather be than in Draven's arms.

[10]
DRAVEN

THE WINDS ARE mild this solar, perfect for travel. Before we left, Galen attempted to show me on his radar where he believes a herd of rogcow are congregating, but I typically trust my instincts on such hunting missions.

My instinct tells me to head north, which is exactly where we're going.

Molly and I take a brisk pace as we walk. We're both wearing zu-gear over our minnasuits and carrying heavy packs on our backs. Mine is slightly heavier, but in order to have all the supplies we'll need, it required her to carry some of the load. Pride thrums through me to see her carry the pack with ease.

"Are you okay, my mate?" I ask through the

comms, stopping to look at her through the glass of her rebreather mask.

Her cheeks are a ruddy red that matches the dirt dusting up around us from her exertion. "I'm perfect." She bites on her bottom lip in a way that has my minnasuit tightening around my cock.

Now is not the time for such activities.

Later, I promise myself.

She blinks with her one eye in the unusual way that I've come to enjoy about her. It's a gesture that seems to agree with my unspoken thoughts.

"We must always keep our eyes on the horizon. Anything that moves could be a threat. I'll eliminate any and all threats as long as you make me aware of them," I say as we continue moving.

I'm headed for the Phyxer Mountains. The mountains themselves are many metalengths into the red, hazy clouds. We're not going to travel up them, though. We're going through the Gunteer Channel—a narrow passageway carved long ago right through the mountain.

Breccan would rekking have my nog on a stick if he knew I was not only planning this, but also taking my prized mate with me.

She is strong.

Together, we are capable.

Not to mention, it is the only way. My instinct tells me the rogcow have herded through the channel, seeking safety from our last massive geostorm. Their normal wandering places have been ravished by the weather.

I point ahead. "See that dark, red shadow?"

"Looks like someone painted a bar down the side of the mountain," she says, her voice breathless.

My brows pinch together as I ascertain whether or not I should relieve her of her pack. We left at sunup this morning and now nearly a half solar has gone without our stopping to rest. I shouldn't push such a rigorous pace, but Sokko's life depends on our hastiness.

"It's a crevasse. A trick of the eyes. When we get closer, you'll see," I tell her. "It's about two metal-engths straight through. The winds are incredibly strong, though. We'll have to tie ourselves together, so we don't get lost in the dust." I take her gloved hand in mine. "You're so brave, Molly mate."

She rewards me with one of her bright smiles that shows all her white, useless teeth. So beautiful. We continue on. As we grow nearer to the Gunteer Channel, the thoughts become loud inside my head. I'm given glimpses of my mother, sending aching stabs into my heart. It makes me wonder about Molly's little

Willow. Only three revolutions old. I know how the little alien feels losing her mother.

"Do you ever think of going to try to find your Willow?" I ask, my voice husky and dry.

She tenses and shakes her nog. "I wouldn't know where to begin, Draven."

"I could help you if that is your wish." I would do anything to make her happy. Even if it means leaving my family to search for hers. "I'm sure Theron would assist as well."

She falls against me, and when her arms squeeze me, I realize it was intentional. A Molly hug. "You're sweet," she says, her head tilting up, so she can see me. "But not only am I lost on a planet I never knew existed, I'm also a wanted criminal." Her brows furrow together. "I've never felt so hopeless about something. All I can do is trust she's happy wherever she is."

As we travel, thoughts of my mother come back to mind.

***

"W-We'll find each other again," Mother rasps. Her eyes are wild as black liquid oozes from the corners, leaving a dark, wet trail as they escape into her hair. "In The Eternals."

Her hands are bound, so she won't claw at her skin anymore. I have to fist my hands to keep from scratching at my own flesh. Whatever Mother has, I think I have it, too.

"Don't leave me," I beg, my voice a mere whisper.

"One d-day I'll be f-free," she croaks, her mind once again slipping into the madness.

"Mother," I whimper.

She coughs, and her entire body shudders. Spittle hits my face. They say she's contagious. I don't know what contagious means. All I know is she's sick.

"Who will feed me, Mother?"

"They will, my heart."

"Who will make sure I'm not cold at night, Mother?"

"They...will..."

"Who will—"

"Free me, beast," she hisses, her fangs bared. "Free me, so I can rip them from my bones!"

My eyes widen. "What, Mother? What's in your bones?"

"THEY ARE INSIDE ME!" she screams, her entire body flailing on the bed.

Panic rises up inside of me. I pull the small magknife that belonged to my father before he went to The Eternals from my belt. My hands shake as I try to saw through the zuta-metal clamp around her wrists.

It's not working!

"Mother," I cry out. "Let me go get—"

"No!" she shouts. "They'll take you from me! I'll suffer alone! No mort should ever suffer alone!"

Liquid heat streaks down my cheeks. I hastily swipe it away and let out a sob when I realize my tears are black like hers.

I'm scared.

Will they bind me, too?

"They're coming," she snarls. "Run, Draven! Run!"

I give my mother one last stare before I scamper off. I've barely made it to the door to swipe my keycard when it rolls open. A mort several years older than me and dressed completely in zu-gear, yanks me up by the arms.

"Let me go!" I wail. "Mother! Mother!"

"Run, Draven!" she calls out.

I squirm in his strong grip. When I see his eyes behind the glass, betrayal cuts me open.

Breccan.

He's always so nice to me and teaches me things. How to hunt. How to scout for danger. How to read. He even looks after little Hadrian now.

But now...

"You're sick," he says, his voice tight with sadness. "We must try and—"

Images of those things inside of me eating away at

my bones suddenly blackens my thoughts. I grow feral in his grip and screech as I squirm to get away. My claws rake along his zu-gear, but don't puncture the material.

He shouts to someone to bring the sedative.

The next few moments are a blur.

Then nothing.

Nothing.

Nothing.

Mother? Are we in The Eternals?

No one answers…

***

"Draven!" Molly cries out, dragging me from the past. "You're trembling. What's wrong?"

My bones buzz with the reminder of the past. The way my bones felt as though things were crawling inside of them, gnawing them hollow. I know I'm free from The Rades, but that disease still haunts me. That disease took my mother.

I look around frantically, trying to place exactly where we are. Anything to steal my attention away from that fateful night when she went to The Eternals and I went to a reform cell.

Maybe not right away.

But eventually.

At first, they tried to treat me.

But then, they simply wanted to keep me away from the others.

Breccan, only eighteen revolutions old, held me when I was too weak. He roared with me when I needed to rage over the injustice of it all. He listened when I needed to talk. I was ten revolutions old, but during those many micro-revolutions, I aged well beyond my years. When the madness became too great to handle, I spent what felt like eons locked away in the dark. Those times still come to me in the form of terrors in the night. I can't shake those memories away no matter how I try.

"Tell me what's wrong," Molly urges.

And with a shaky sigh, I do.

We walk, and I talk. I tell her of my mother—before the dreadful disease took her. I tell her of watching her suffer. I tell her of my own suffering. The pain still ravages my heart, and this, too, I tell her. By the time I've finished, we've reached the mouth of the crevasse, and Molly is sobbing.

"Don't cry, my mate," I rumble. "I do not wish to push my anguish into your arms."

She gives me a Molly mate hug. The sort of hug that seeps deep inside of me. It chases away the lingering shadows. Brightens places that have never seen light.

"Your anguish is a part of you, Draven. Just like my anguish is a part of me. I'm not crying because you upset me. I'm crying *for* you, Draven. For all you've gone through and what you lost," she says, her voice shaky.

I rest my visor's glass against hers, so I can see her lovely face. We share a moment before I pull away and hunt for my rope. After tethering us together, I clench my jaw as I worry about the travel through this channel.

"Stay behind me, and cut anything that comes near us," I instruct. "I'll cover us from the front."

"We've got this, boo."

I don't know what a boo is, but my mate likes to make up names for me. I think of them as her hug words. Like verbal squeezes to my heart. They affect me all the same. Lift me up and power me to continue on.

With my mate, I'll always keep moving forward.

The shadows don't own me anymore.

I have my very own sun in the dark, chasing away the monsters.

[11]
MOLLY

It's like trying to walk through a tornado.

Impossible.

But, somehow, with Draven leading the way, anything seems possible.

I tuck my chin down and force one foot in front of the other. My thighs tremble under the strain, and I've given up trying to moderate my breathing. I'm sure Draven can hear my heaving over the comms, but if he does, he doesn't mention it.

The red-orange dust obliterates most of the light, and what little is left is hazy-red, battering my protective visor. It amazes me how the morts have survived on this brutal planet for so long when every inch of it seems designed to wipe out life instead of help sustain it. I grasp the tether more firmly at the thought and keep pushing forward. One step at a time.

That's how I've survived so far.

One step at a time.

Thinking the word survive has the memory of meeting Draven for the first time springing to the forefront. I begin to hum the song again without thinking as we trek on, the journey seemingly endless. I don't realize it for a few minutes, but Draven begins to sing along with me, his voice sure and baritone.

Of course, it doesn't take long before the exertion is too strenuous to keep singing, but I hum along with Draven with every step, focusing on the words, the melody, instead of the endlessness.

"Watch your nog!" Draven shouts suddenly, then reaches back, shoving my head down between my legs. Exhausted from the strain, my legs buckle, and I fold into a crouch.

"What is it?" I yell once I catch my breath.

Once the danger has passed, Draven carefully helps me to my feet. As he checks my suit and gear for damage, he explains, "Rocks, debris from the mountain that broke off during the geostorms. We must be careful. If I tell you to get down, you get down without hesitating. Will you do this for me?"

His voice is urgent, pleading. Recognizing his

desperation as fear for my safety, I nod. "Of course. As long as you don't put yourself in any danger either."

Draven leans closer to press the face of his gear against mine. I close my eyes and imagine him holding me like he had the night before. "I have no desire to meet The Eternals, Molly. Not anymore."

I read the gravity of his words in his eyes and tears spring to mine before I push the rush of emotion down and back. Not now. I couldn't save my own child, but I will save Aria's. "Later," I tell him. "Let's get out of this mess, and then we'll do the dirty."

Draven winces comically. "Dirty?" he asks with a shudder. "Must we?"

Despite the precariousness of our situation and the constant howl and threat from the flying rocks, I laugh. "Sex, Draven. Sex."

He quirks his head then turns around. "We morts do not like getting dirty. Dirt contains germs and can be dangerous. But I agree that mating can sometimes be so." He glances over his shoulder and gives me a heated look. "I'll get dirty, but only for you, my mate."

"Then, let's get going and get to the other side."

We travel for hours more, dodging missiles of jagged rock. Out of nowhere, Draven is struck by a boulder the size of a small squirrel. He flips, ass over tea kettle, and lands some dozen feet away, still for a few long, heart-wrenching moments. Still holding the tether, I inch my way toward his still body, my heart in my throat.

When I reach him, I huddle down and shake his shoulder. "Draven?" I say over the comms. "Draven, are you okay?"

He doesn't respond. My heart lurches into my throat. "Draven!"

"Mortarekker, I must be getting old. I couldn't move fast enough."

I melt over him like a pile of hot wax. "You scared me. Are you hurt?"

"My pride is a bit bruised, but I am well." Holding the tether for balance, he gets to his feet with a groan. "We must keep going, or we'll be here when it gets dark."

"Oh no, uh-uh, no, sir. We're not going anywhere if you're hurt. We can find somewhere to stay for the night and let you rest."

Draven gestures around us at our dusty surroundings. "Where would you suggest? The vacuu-pod would blow away in seconds. We must keep going."

He starts to leave again, and I plant my feet until he looks back at me in frustration. "We will keep going until we find a suitable place for shelter, and then we'll stop for the night." When he glares at me, I add,

"Either we find a place for shelter or I'll sit my happy ass down right here and won't move another inch."

Instead of getting mad, like I expect, Draven smiles at me, which makes me a little uneasy until he says, "My mate is a fighter. I like this. Fine. We'll keep going until we find a suitable place for the vacuu-pod."

I didn't really expect him to agree with me, so he's already gone several feet ahead by the time I catch up with him. The winds seem to increase in intensity the longer the day grows until we're nearly leaning forward to touch the ground in the effort to keep upright. Each step only brings us precious inches forward, and I'm already regretting my stubbornness. Finding shelter in this desolate place when we can barely see will be next to impossible.

Eventually Draven directs me to inspect the right side of the crevasse while he canvases the left. Unable to see through the thick sheets of dust, I have to rely on touch through the padded gloves. Even holding my hand out to palpate the rock walls on my side proves difficult with the gusting wind, but I force myself to do it.

For Draven.

I'm humming another song to myself some time later when my hand suddenly disappears into nothingness, and I fall to the side, pushed by momentum and the relentless gusts. A scream tears from my throat as I tumble into darkness and crash to the ground with a breath-stealing *flump*.

The comms fill with Draven's shouted, "Molllyyyyy!"

My bones and joints aching from the impact, I lie there for a moment until I get my bearings. When I can speak, I say, "I'm okay, but I think I've found our cave."

"Stay there," Draven instructs. "I'm coming."

As I wait for him to backtrack and reach the opening of the cave, I look around to see where exactly *there* is. It's less of a cave and more of a passageway, really. A crevasse inside the crevasse. The floor is covered in inches of the red-orange dust and the walls are a solid granite-looking rock of ebony, glossy and glittering with shards of lighter rock. A blue light beckons from the far end of the passage, a beacon in all the crimson.

Draven joins me a short while later. "Are you all right?" Before I can answer, he's crossing the small space to my side where he carefully inspects my suit. I wait patiently until he's done, understanding his need for reassurance. "You've done well."

"I don't think this first room is big enough for the vacuu-pod, but if we follow the passage, we may find a bigger opening, and we'll get farther away from all the dust."

"Follow me," he says, heading toward the blue light.

We make our way to the back of the passage, leaving the howling red glow from the crevasse behind. "What is this blue light?" I ask. "Have you ever seen anything like it before?"

"I don't know, but we'll be careful in case there is anything dangerous. I will protect you." He retrieves his zonnoblaster from his pack and holds it at the ready.

I don't think I'll ever get tired of hearing him say he'll take care of me. I can protect myself, but it's comforting to know I don't have to do everything alone. With Draven as my mate, I won't ever have to be alone again.

The deeper we go into the mountain, the brighter the blue light glows. Dual threads of apprehension and excitement weave themselves inside me. It could be some sort of ship. Maybe we could use it to find Willow. I dismiss the thought before it can completely form. Willow is gone. There will be no saving her.

"Don't worry, my mate. These caves feel abandoned."

"I'm not worried," I answer.

"You were singing your La-La song over the comms," Draven responds.

"I was not," I snap.

"You always La-La when you're feeling anxious. There's no need. We would have seen signs of other life if there were something living here."

"I do not sing when I'm anxious."

"That's true," he says as we round a curve and then another. "You sing when you're happy, when you're sad, when you're working. Except you sing different tunes with each mood. You're my little songbird."

"Shut it, Lieutenant, and keep walking."

"Yes, mate," he answers, and even though I can't see his face, I can hear the smile in his voice over the comms.

When there is no more dust and the sound of the howling wind can no longer be heard, Draven comes to an abrupt stop. I slam into his back, but his great form doesn't even jolt.

"What is it?" I ask. Then, I look around his shoulder and gasp.

The passageway dead-ends at an immense cavern filled will brilliant turquoise water.

"A pool!"

A beautiful, glimmering pool. After the long, dusty walk through the crevasse and days of staring at the barren, desert-like landscape of the planet surrounding the facility, I'd almost forgotten how beautiful water can be. The blue glow seems to be emanating from the water itself.

I automatically go to take a step toward it when Draven tugs at my arm. "What? It's gorgeous."

"We don't know if it's contaminated. Before we do anything, let's set up the vacuu-pod, and I'll measure the R-levels."

With a mournful look at the shimmering pool, I follow Draven across the cavern to a smooth patch of gravel beach deep inside. As Draven sets up the vacuu-pod, I study our surroundings and find the pool of water isn't the only thing different. I'd been so distracted by the water, I didn't notice the myriad of plant life blooming from the most unlikely places. Cracks in the black rock. Streamers of dark blue seaweed fluttering under the surface.

Once Draven finishes setting up the vacuu-pod, he joins me, also in awe of the cavern. "I've never seen anything like this."

"You've never been here before?" I ask, stepping closer to the pool.

"We tend to stick near to facility. It's safer." He pulls a device out of his pack. "Let me check the R-levels here."

"Are you sure I can't go swimming?"

"Not unless you want to catch a disease."

I slump and sit at the entrance of the vacuu-pod as I watch him take samples from the gravel, the water, the air, and even the plant life. He shakes his head each time, his brow furrowed.

"What is it?"

"This place...it's as though it's untouched. Life flourishes here. These plants, this water, I've never seen R-levels so low. I have to take these samples back for Galen to study. I don't know what it means, but he will."

When he's finished, I tug him inside the vacuu-pod. As much as I want to take a dip in the pool, we have a goal and we're both exhausted. "Maybe we can come back to take more samples. Bring Galen to study. If he gives the okay, maybe we can even come back to go swimming. The dust storm out there would be worth it if we could go swimming."

"You are fearless, aren't you, Molly mate?" Draven says as he pulls off both of our gear.

"Only with you," I answer.

In minutes we're bundled in the thin blankets, Draven tucking me under his chin and pulling me close. "And I with you," I hear before succumbing to sleep.

[12]
DRAVEN

I WAKE WARM—TOO warm—and with my cock hard. Judging by the way I feel, I would say we've only been asleep for a few hours. I doubt the sun has come up yet. I should go back to sleep, but then I realize why my cock is hard. Hot lips kiss the side of my neck as my mate strokes at me through my unders.

"You must get some rest," I murmur, my voice thick from sleep.

Her words are warm against my neck. "I'll rest better if I'm...you know..."

"Relaxed from the toxica?"

"Yes. My mind is racing."

I roll her onto her back and kiss her in the blue glow from the nearby pool that's visible through the window of our small vacuu-pod. It takes some wriggling, but we manage to undress completely. There's not much room to service her like I wish with my mouth, so I have to settle for my fingers. I retract my claws as not to hurt her and massage her nub that vibrates with need. Easily, I work her up into a state that has her crying out my name. Then, I press the head of my thickness against her slick opening. With a hard push of my hips, I drive all the way into the depths of my mate. Her body is tight, hot, and hugs me in a way that makes me nearly feral with the need to claim her with my seed.

A snarl leaves my lips as I buck into her. Her useless claws scratch at my scarred skin and moans rip from her throat. I attack her supple lips, relishing in the sweet taste of her. She likes sliding her tongue in between the groove of my forked tongue, which seems to make my cock twitch with delight.

"Oh God," she whimpers. "Harder."

I slam into her with a desperate fury. Her nog thunks against the vacuu-pod wall, making her giggle. With each laugh, her cunt clenches around me.

Not ready.

I'm not done devouring her.

My lips find her neck, and I suckle her skin there. She whines when my fangs scrape along her flesh. The urge to bite her is nearly overwhelming. All of Calix's and Avrell's training is at the forefront of my mind. Diseases. Pathogens. Germs. None of that matters with Molly. If she has something, I want it too. Where she goes, I go. Even to The Eternals.

"Harderharderharder," she chants, her fingers sliding into my hair. She tugs at it and cries out, "Do it."

My mind grows black with lust and need as my fangs pierce her flesh. She moans loudly, her feet digging into my backside. The moment her blood floods across my tongue, I feel as though The Rades has overtaken me again. But instead of those monsters inside my nog, it's my mate's sweet moans that fill me up. I suck at the wound I've made before pulling away, so I can look at her. She cradles my cheeks with her palms and locks eyes with me. We remain transfixed on one another until my sac seizes up in pleasure, and I explode with my release. My cock spurts out every drop of my seed, filling my mate with what I hope is a little mortling of our own one solar.

The toxica hits her blood stream, and her grip on my cheeks slips. I pull out, my cock still leaking at the tip, and take hold of her wrists. I kiss the insides of her palms. One and then the other. Then, I pin her arms down as I rain kisses down on her perfect face. She lets out a content sigh. Her eyes aren't wild or confused. She's sated and happy.

I did this.

I pleased my mate.

Kiss after kiss, I reassure her she's mine, and I'll always take care of her. Eventually, I grow tired again and settle beside her. The last thing I remember before falling asleep is her fingertips gently brushing along my scars as she regained her movement after the toxica.

"Rest my mate," she whispers.

***

Away from the refuge of the crevasse hidden in the mountain, my mind begins to clear some. The taboo feeling of what I did with Molly doesn't seem to fade. If anything, I feel worse by the second. If Breccan and the others find out I bit my mate...

Images of the reform cell below the facility make me shudder.

I won't go back.

Molly wouldn't allow it.

That thought soothes me. She's a fighter, my mate. Brave and resilient and beautiful. She is the sun, she is the sky, she is my everything.

And she tastes so rekking good.

I look over my shoulder and give her a wave. She

grins through her mask and waves back. The winds are calmer this solar, but still brutal. Once reassured she's still behind me, I keep trekking forward. I can't help but think about the moment her blood hit my tongue. Sweet. So sweet. When we woke later, I'd felt shamed by the blood-crusted holes in her neck. All four of them. She'd simply gingerly touched them, her cheeks turning pink, telling me I was a kinky bastard. Whatever the rekk a kinky bastard is.

Alas, it is true.

I am this kinky bastard.

Because the scene keeps replaying in my mind over and over. It makes my cock hard in my minnasuit beneath my zu-gear. Images of holding her down and biting her in other less conspicuous places has me groaning with need. Again, I look over my shoulder to make sure she's safe. When our eyes meet, she's no longer smiling.

Fear.

Pure, unfiltered fear.

She points past me, her hand shaking against the wind.

It's her scream that does me in.

"DRAVEN!"

I've unsheathed my magknife and have already whipped around in time to see a sabrevipe tearing along the channel toward us. He's large—fat even—and I wonder what he's been feeding on to keep him so plump. His size is to my advantage, though.

"Stay along the wall," I roar to Molly as I cut through our link. I'll need to be free to take down this massive beast.

"Draven!" she cries out as her body hits the dirt.

Now that we're no longer tethered together, I prowl toward the sabrevipe that has stopped just ahead of me. It claws at the dirt and snarls at me. My eyes flicker up the side of the mountain wall.

One. Two. Three.

I count the handholds at my disposal. I'll have to be quick. I cannot fail because if I do, it'll get past me to my mate.

Over my rekking dead body.

I charge forward, my eyes on the beast while keeping the wall in my periphery. As soon as I'm close to the first handhold, I grab at it. I hoist myself up, my feet digging into the side of the mountain, then I hop to the next one that's a little higher. Beneath me, the sabrevipe growls in confusion. I've just grabbed the third handhold when it darts its head back toward my cowering mate.

No.

Not happening, fat rekk.

I drop from the handhold, so I land on the beast. It's pink, hairless skin gets pierced with my magknife as my other arm wraps around its neck. It bucks, trying to shake me off, but I'm already pulling my magknife out again to stab it. Over and over in between its ribs. When it weakens and stumbles, I use my weight to force it down into submission. I land a fatal blow of my magknife into its ear.

As soon as I'm certain it's dead, I rise from its unmoving body and stalk after my mate. With a growl, I pick up the end of the rope in the dirt and roughly pull her to me. She stumbles but then rushes forward to keep up with my pulling. Once she lands hard against my chest, I let out a sigh of relief.

"You're safe now," I rumble, squeezing her tight.

"Draven, you scared the shit out of me," she whimpers. "I thought you were going to die."

"We all go to The Eternals eventually, my mate. But not this rekking solar."

She pulls away slightly, and I tie us back together. The end is in sight, and after not too much longer, I pull her out of the mouth of the Gunteer Channel.

The winds are gone now that we're out of the crevasse that seems to suck air. What lies beyond confuses me.

A valley.

A green valley.

I blink several times as I try to process the herds of rogcow munching on mosshay. It grows plentiful here. Even some trees I've never seen before grow within the valley, some ripe with fruit.

Did the sabrevipe eat me?

Have I gone to The Eternals?

This is certainly unlike The Graveyard or any place I've ever seen on Mortuus.

"It's beautiful," Molly whispers. "And the cows are here. Sokko will have his milk." She lets out a tearful sob of relief as she unties the rope and walks forward to the nearest herd. Typically, the rogcows scatter when they see us morts coming, but not these. These beasts seem oblivious to the predator before them. They feed on the mosshay without care. Several ronk nearby.

"These are...different," she utters, a small chuckle escaping her. "Never seen white cows with red eyes before."

One in particular looks right at her and ronks.

"Your rogcows don't look like this?"

She shakes her head. "For one, our cows have four legs, not eight." Her hand tentatively reaches out, and she pats the rear of one of the beasts. "And they don't have two tails." It lifts its head and nudges her with its snout. "Or, weird, one eye."

Her rogcows must look strange as these look how they always do. Fatter, though. My mouth waters just thinking of sinking my teeth into a meaty thigh and—

"Stop growling or you'll scare Eye-lean away."

She enunciates each part of the name. I cock my nog in confusion.

"Eye-lean."

The rogcow in question ronks loudly at me.

"Look, one eye," Molly says, "and she leans in when you pet her. Cute, huh?"

Cute is not the word I prefer.

Delicious, perhaps.

"I can slaughter Eye-lean and check her R-Levels. By sundown, we can feast on this—"

Ronnnnnk!

"Draven, no," she growls. My mate is fierce in this moment.

I arch a brow. "Why not?"

"Because she's our pet now! You don't eat pets, babe." She pats the beast's head. "Stop looking at her like she's food. It hurts her feelings. Eye-lean is a part of our family now."

I suppress a groan, but I do what my mate wills. With

a resigned sigh, I slowly approach the animal. I'm surprised that it doesn't run from me. Instead, it leans into my touch, too. I roam my palm along her fattened sides.

"She is pregnant," I tell her.

"Awww," she coos. "Then we have to keep her. She'll provide us with the milk she needs, and in favor, we can protect her from those scary cat things. I will take care of the calf. I know how to deliver calves. Did it back home when I was a teenager." Her bright, hopeful brown eyes meet mine. "Please, handsome. Can we keep her?"

"If that is your wish, my mate."

Perhaps we can eat one of Eye-lean's ronking friends instead.

[13]
MOLLY

ROOOOOOOONK.

The rogcow ambles between the two of us, securely latched to the tether, but I follow a couple steps behind like a worried mother. I missed having animals to take care of, to tend to. Maybe it's my mothering instinct in overdrive.

The red-orange dust seems to be easier to deal with now that we're going with the flow rather than against it. It allows at least a modicum of visibility which allows me to notice every time Draven looks back, his fangs practically dripping with drool.

"Stop looking at Eileen like you want to take a bite out of her. The milk she'll provide to everyone is more than enough reason to keep her alive. Not to mention the benefits for Sokko. Plus, if we go back for a male rogcow, we can keep breeding them for a herd. Maybe that Oz guy can make a pen for them. I was good at taking care of cows back home when I was younger. Eventually, we may not even have to hunt for them. We can raise some for breeding and milk and some for meat."

"You mean to keep the animals in cages?" Draven asks.

"Well, no. I mean sort of. What you do is build a large pen, so they can walk around and eat. Hmm. There isn't much green space like there was on the other side of the crevasse. We'll have to talk to the others about the best way to do it. Maybe we can build the pen in that grassy area and go back and forth."

Roooooooonk, Eileen bellows as though she agrees with me.

"Plus, if we do that, it'll give us another opportunity to stay in the caves by the lake. Maybe I'll even convince you to let me go swimming."

I don't have to see his face to know he's frowning. For being badass vampire aliens, these morts sure are afraid of anything they don't know or understand. I guess losing everyone you love will make you hesitant of new experiences. I can certainly relate to that.

"We'll do no such thing until it's been thoroughly tested," Draven says.

I roll my eyes at his back. He'd said the same thing the second night we stayed in the cavern with Eileen on our way back through the crevasse. As we tromp through the dusty, windy path, I wish I had convinced him to let me take a little dip. A swim in the gorgeous, clear turquoise water sounds heavenly at this point.

If we weren't on such a time squeeze getting Eileen here back to Sokko, I would have convinced Draven to stay another day or two to explore. As it is, we're moving at nearly double the speed, the fastest Eileen will allow, down the tunnel toward the facility. Thankfully, it's much easier to travel with the forceful wind at our backs. Even with Eileen, we make good time.

By early afternoon, we emerge from Gunteer Channel at the base of the Phyxer Mountains. The last time we'd traveled, it had taken the better part of a day, but I know we're quickly running out of time. If we hurry, we should make it by full dark. The vast desert stretches out in front of us, seemingly endless, but we have a life to save, and though I couldn't protect my own child, I will protect Sokko. It's with the thought of my sweet Willow cradled in my mind that I tug Eileen's chain and follow Draven out of the mountains and across the desert.

We travel for many hours. Soon, I forget what it's

like to not be moving forward. Eileen ambles alongside me as though she doesn't have a care in the world. Her loud bellows are lost in the rumbles from the ever-present geostorm clouds and constant thunder.

Thunder that seems to grow louder with each step.

Great. The last thing we need is to be caught in the middle of a storm.

"Are we going to get caught in that?" I ask Draven over the rumble.

"No, my mate. We will be safe inside the facility before any storms hit as long as we keep going."

The thunder roars.

"Draven? Are you sure?"

A loud mechanical shriek roars over his answer.

"Draven?"

The thunder sounds closer. Like it's right on top of us. Eileen *rooooooonks* loudly, and instinct has me whirling around.

A large vehicle is almost right on top of us. I shriek and throw myself on top of Eileen who bellows in protest. Draven whirls around at the last second and, spotting the vehicle, lunges to the side to avoid being run over.

The vehicle rocks to a stop. Draven crab-crawls across the stony earth to my side. Eileen tugs at the lead, but I keep my hand tight around the rope.

"Draven? Who is that? Is it one of the other morts?"

But Draven doesn't answer. He's already on his feet with his zonnoblaster at the ready, pointed at the driver's side door. "Open up, and show yourself."

The door creaks open, and something flies out in our direction. A second later, it explodes. A grenade or a bomb? Oh my God!

"Arrrrrrrghhhhh!" Draven screams, slumping to the ground.

"No!" I shout.

With Eileen bawling madly, I scramble on the ground to where Draven fell, finding him in a silent heap a few feet away. "Please please please please."

Draven coughs and sits up. "Get behind me," he orders before bringing his gun up again. To the person —or whatever it is—behind the door, he says, "Come out! Slowly."

"Is that you, Phalix? I've been looking for you."

Phalix?

Draven shoots to his feet so fast it's as though one second he's sitting and the next, he's standing. A man steps down from the vehicle, one who looks like a mort, like Draven when he's in the throes of madness, but worse. So, so much worse.

No outer gear. No mask. Just walking about freely,

breathing the air like it's not going to kill him at any second.

"Phalix?" Draven says, the tip of the gun dipping. Then realization dawns. "Lox? You crazy mortarekker. What the rekk do you think you're doing? How have you survived since you left Sector 1779? And without your zu-gear or rebreather?"

Sector 1779. Where Emery and Calix had encountered that mad mort who'd killed Calix's father. The mad mort who was now holding a gun at the both of us. When Draven told me about what happened with them, I'd been horrified.

"Never mind that," Lox says. "The two of you will take me to the facility."

"You're not going anywhere near the facility," Draven growls. "Calix told us what you did. That you tried to kill him and his mate. Stay where you are. If you come any closer, I'll blast your rekking nog off without another thought. But if you come quietly, I will speak with Breccan to figure out what we can do with you, so no one has to get hurt."

"You think I care about Breccan? He's just as bad as Phalix, leaving me on this planet to rot. You don't give me orders, you do what I say. Or like I did with Calix, I'll take your pretty little alien mate and leave you for the sabrevipes." He motions toward us with his gun. "Now you'll give me the female. She can ride with me while you and the rogcow lead the way to the facility."

I see the internal struggle on Draven's face. "It's fine," I tell him. "I'll go with him."

"The rekk you will," Draven growls. *Crack crack crack.* The sub-bones in his neck begin to straighten, and his ears squash against his head.

"We have to get back to the mortling," I insist, passing Draven Eileen's lead. I take a step closer to Lox and the vehicle. The only way we'll get out of this is for me to take myself out of the equation. Draven and the rogcow are the most important things. "I can take care of myself."

"Enough," Lox shouts. He snatches me by the arm, and I let him pull me to his side. "She's coming with me whether you like it or not."

"No," comes a new voice, "she's not."

Then all hell breaks loose.

Lox grips my arms and positions me in front of him. Two figures emerge from the shadows, and my bones turn to jelly when I recognize Calix and Emery from the other's descriptions. Emery's about the size of Eileen, not that I'd tell her that. What the hell was Calix thinking, dragging her out here?

"Calix," Lox says as though greeting an old friend. "I thought I left you for dead."

"You wish, old mort," Calix replies. "Let her go, or we'll make you let her go. You tried this once already, and you failed. You'll fail again because our mates are our family, and no one, not even you, will harm them."

"I was your family!" Lox shouts. "And you left me for dead."

"We would have rescued you, but you've spent too much time on your own. You've lost what little sense you had, if any. Let's work this out, so no one has to get hurt. There are morts counting on us." Draven takes tentative steps closer.

Lox raises his gun threateningly. "No. You think I care about you when you've shown me such disregard?"

Then Eileen is running, but not away from us. She charges toward Lox, who is still shouting, not realizing the rogcow is aiming straight for him. She headbutts him directly in the stomach, causing him to fall in the ground. Her powerful hooves—all freaking eight of them—trample over his emaciated body. I close my eyes at the sound of bones snapping.

When it's over, I crack my eyelids and find Eileen at the rear of the vehicle, inching her way back toward me, her one red eye blinking solemnly. I lift a hand and say, "Shh, girl. It's okay. Come here, sweet, brave girl, I've got you."

Calix and Draven crouch over Lox's still body. Blood leaks from the corner of his mouth, his eyes still wide-open, looking at the sky.

"He's dead," Calix announces, his eyes on his very pregnant wife, who visibly relaxes at the news. "We'll take his body back and give him a proper burial. He may have been mad, but he was a mort."

They cover him with a blanket from Draven's pack and load him in the back of Lox's vehicle. It's not big enough to transport Eileen, so they tie her to the back. I guess we'll drive as slow as she can walk. Emery and Calix load up in the vehicle they had repaired from Sector 1779 and drive ahead of us.

"Emery is leaking colostrum. We hope that combined with the rogcow milk, it will satisfy little Sokko. We'll ride ahead and update the others."

When we're alone, Draven turns to me. "Don't ever do that again," he says, pulling me into his arms. "My brave, sweet mate. You took the life straight from my heart."

I squeeze him tight. "Does this mean you'll let me keep Eileen instead of eating her?" I ask.

[14]
DRAVEN

"Her name is Eye-lean, and no, you can't eat her!" Molly gripes, swatting away Hadrian's hand as he reaches for her rogcow.

Her rogcow.

That's the absolute truth.

My mate treats that walking, ronking, meaty beast as though it's her very own mortling. I'm beyond salivating over it because she made me see reason.

We need it for Sokko.

The rogcow ronks and kicks out her hind legs as Theron hoses her down in the large Decontamination Bay. Galen's already checked her R-Levels, took a sample, and bounded off to the lab with Avrell and Calix. She's clean, and frankly, edible. But most importantly her milk is safe for them to work on a special formula for the mortling.

"But you say there's more?" Hadrian probes. "A whole herd?"

The starved glint in his eyes has Molly whacking at him again.

"They're her family. Go eat some green bunches, and leave her cousins alone!"

Hadrian chuckles, clearly amused at riling my mate up. I give him a fierce glare that has him slinking away to pester someone else.

"We need to see Avrell," I urge Molly. "He's expecting us back to check us over."

She goes back to arguing with Hadrian, and I rub at my temple. When Lox threw the handheld explosive, I'd been knocked on my rump. Hit my nog pretty hard on the ground. Ever since, I've been slightly dizzy, and the throbbing is incessant.

"Hey," Molly coos, suddenly close, both hands sliding to my cheeks. "You don't look so well. Let's get out of here. I've threatened Hadrian's life if he so much as dares look at Eye-lean funny."

I simply nod at her and allow her to guide us out of the Decontamination Bay. We walk down the hall to the medical bay and into Avrell's lab.

"Ahh, there you are," Avrell says, giving us a tired smile.

"Check to make sure my mate is safe," I grumble. "Please."

Molly shakes her nog. "I'm fine. But you're not fine. Hop up on that table, and let Doc have a look at you."

Begrudgingly, I sit on the table before stretching my body out. The lights are bright, and I wince against them. Avrell's brows furrow as he sets to running a series of tests on me.

"Draven."

I blink away my daze and find Molly seated on the edge of the table, holding my hand. "Mmm?"

"He said you have a concussion, and you need to stay awake. Come on, big boy," she says. "Sit up."

"The dizziness and confusion will come and go," Avrell says. "I'd like you to stay awake until it's time for bed. Just so we can make sure nothing strange occurs. But with rest, you should be fine. I'll give you some ghan-dust tablets."

"What are ghan-dust tablets?" Molly asks.

"Ghan are rock-like roots found in the underground wells that can be ground to dust and used for certain ailments," Avrell explains. "Like rekking nog-aches."

I swallow the ghan-dust tablets dry and shoot Avrell a firm look that says, "My mate. Now."

Instead of chuckling, per Avrell's usual demeanor, he simply nods, his lips forming a firm line. Worrying over Sokko is taking its toll on him.

I slide off the table then pick my mate up. She lets out a little squeal until I set her down on the table.

"I'm not hurt," she says with a huff. "I'm tired and sore, but just fine."

Avrell bypasses the machines he used to check me over. After a quick scan to check her R-Levels—which are thankfully not present—he grabs the wegloscan. I tense and lock eyes with him. Hope flutters inside my stomach, not helping my dizziness whatsoever. Molly is completely oblivious to Avrell's intent.

Please...

Please...

Please...

Days ago, I would've laughed if I saw myself standing here silently begging. Now, I'm not laughing. I'm rekking hoping.

Avrell waves the wegloscan over her abdomen, and it beeps. A green light flashes. Both Avrell and I let out a sharp breath.

"What?" Molly demands, her voice shrill.

"Are you certain?" I ask Avrell.

He nods rapidly, a smile stretching across his face. "The wegloscan is one hundred percent accurate. One hundred percent, Draven. This means—"

I wave off his words. "My mate and I need a moment."

He frowns but acquiesces. "I'm going to peek in on Calix and Galen to see how the formula is coming along. I'll be back to check on you both."

As soon as he leaves, Molly regards me with tears welling in her pretty brown eyes. I stroke my claw gently along her jaw.

"When I was locked in a reform cell, I was hopeless, Molly. Everything was so dark and painful and horrifying." I squeeze my eyes shut, shuddering at the memory. "I barely made it through. The Rades not only ravished my mind and my body, but it shredded my soul."

A tear leaks out of her eye, and her bottom lip wobbles. "Oh, Draven..."

"But then, hope came in the form of a beautiful alien with a voice of magic," I tell her, astonishment in my tone. "She stumbled right into my arms. As though she were my gift. A gift I didn't know I wanted until I realized it's all I ever wanted."

She sniffles and swipes away the wetness on her cheeks.

"With your smiles and your hugs and your fierce disposition, you threaded those pieces back together with you, Molly, my mate. We're completely woven together now. Together, we're stronger than we ever were apart." I pull her palm to my mouth and kiss her flesh. "We both know unimaginable loss. And through our mutual pain, something wonderful has grown between us."

"Do you really think?" she whispers as her other palm splays over her stomach.

"One hundred percent certain," I tell her. "It is our gift."

More tears leak out.

"But I'm a terrible mother," she rasps out, choking on a sob. "I let them take my little girl. She is three years old, Draven. Lost. Out there without her mother."

"She lives in your heart," I assure her. "And she will live in the heart of our mortling because we will make sure our little one knows all about sweet Willow."

She sits up and throws her arms around my neck, pulling me to her. My nog-ache subsides as my heart thrums wildly in my chest.

"We can do this," she says as though she's trying to assure herself more than me. "Together."

"You're rekking right we will. Never apart. Just like how you insisted trekking through The Graveyard with me on a rogcow hunt. I'll keep trekking through this life with you until one day we meet The Eternals together."

She laughs and kisses my neck. "You're so dark sometimes, but I understand the sentiment. And I love you too. Until the end, baby."

"And then some, my mate."

***

"Explain it to me again," Galen says, marveling at my words.

I go through all of our findings. The cave. The valley. All the plants that seemed to be thriving in our otherwise harsh climate. I brought back some samples, and I've never seen Galen grin so much in all my life.

"You know what this means," Galen tells Breccan. "I'm going to Gunteer Channel."

I expect Breccan to argue, but he gives him a clipped nod. I think he'd agree to anything right now. His son suckles from a nipple—fashioned from the same material our minnasuits are made from—that's attached to a rogstud horn. Between the supplement Calix created from Emery's colostrum, mixed with the rogcow milk, Sokko is finally getting the nutrients he needs. It's been three solars since we came back from our journey, and the little mortling is finally growing. For a spell there, everyone was certain he wouldn't make it.

"Boo," Aria says, sneaking up behind me.

I jolt in surprise and glower at her. Now that I have Molly, my mind isn't a mess. I don't fret about shadows and darkness and bad memories. I don't count exits or have to keep open spaces behind me. All I see is Molly. When my eyes are open and when they are closed. She has cured me.

"How's my little piggy?" she coos as she comes to stand in front of her mate.

Breccan kisses Sokko's head. "Hungry."

"Well, good news," she says with a slightly crazed laugh. "My milk came in. I'm leaking like a damn rogcow. So engorged now. Let me see him."

When she tugs at her minnasuit to reveal a breast, Galen makes a choking sound, and I drop my gaze to the floor. Breccan growls, and his sub-bones start cracking.

"Oh my God, Breccan," Aria chides. "I'm not getting naked for your friends. I'm about to feed our very hungry baby. You're going to have to get that protectiveness in check. You all are. You're breeding us females left and right. Where we come from, the women feed their babies whenever and wherever. I won't cover myself or hide because you think someone might catch a peek."

Breccan growls as he hands Sokko over. "Yes, Madam Commander." His voice is tight, and I nearly chuckle as he uses his body as a shield anyway to protect her from Galen's curious stare.

I leave them to seek out my mate. She's sitting in the sub-faction chatting with Emery and Sayer. Jareth is in a chair nearby with his long legs stretched out in front of him as he fiddles with a piece of metal. It's a thick ring and it makes me realize that both Aria and Emery wear something smaller but similar proclaiming they are taken by their mates. I stalk over to him.

"I need that," I growl.

He lifts a brow. "My cock ring?"

My jaw unhinges slightly. "W-What?"

"This is my cock ring. You need it?"

I take a step back. "I need for you or Oz to make me a zuta-metal ring for my mate. She is mine, and I want everyone to know it."

Jareth laughs. "Oh, we all know it. We know it all night long. You never let us forget it."

When I growl again, he holds up a hand in surrender.

"Don't worry, Lieutenant, I'll get you one."

I give him a nod of thanks. Then, I tilt my nog to the side, curious about his cock ring. "What's it for?"

He straightens in his chair and tears his gaze from mine to look down at it. "Just looks rekking awesome."

"You wear it around it?"

He scoffs. "You think my cock is that small? It's a piercing, Draven." He makes a motion of pinching his claws of one hand and indicates on his other finger where it goes.

He pretends to poke a hole through the tip of his cock.

No.

Who would do such a thing?

I stumble back, my stomach roiling in disgust. "Why?" I demand.

His shoulders shrug. "It feels good."

"Feels good with what? You don't even have a mate."

Pop! Pop! Pop!

His sub-bones start cracking as he jumps to his feet. Calm Jareth is now snarling at me. Does he suffer from The Rades? What is this madness?

Molly's arms wrap around me from behind, and Sayer steps between us to break up a would-be altercation.

"Molly needs a nap," Sayer tells me. "Why don't you go on and take her back to your quarters?"

Jareth glowers at me from over Sayer's shoulder. I frown in confusion but give him a nod. Jareth storms off without another glance back. Sayer claps a hand down on my shoulder.

"Don't worry," he says. "I'll go check on him. He's had a rough time at it lately." He offers his elbow to Emery, who stands nearby with a worried look on her face. "I can escort you back to Calix if you want the company."

She leaves with him, and my mate comes around to stand in front of me.

"You're tired?" I ask her, brushing her hair from her pretty face.

Her grin is devious. "No, I just wanted an excuse to get some alone time with you. Plus, I heard toxica is good for the baby." She waggles her eyebrows at me.

I don't give her an answer.

Just scoop my mate into my arms and run straight for our quarters, nearly knocking down a few morts on our trek.

Her laughter forever chases away any lingering darkness.

She is my light, my mate, my future, my love.

Mine.

[15]

MOLLY

THREE WEEKS LATER

"That's good," I call out. "Take it nice and easy, don't spook her. Hold your lasso up at the ready. In a few seconds, toss it how I taught you, and aim for Eileen's head—nog." I'm still getting used to the alien lingo. "She might be angry at first, but hold steady like you do when you're hunting the sabrevipes."

Hadrian raises the braided rope Ozias and I had manufactured for this specific purpose. He'd shed his shirt at the beginning of our practice when the brilliant Mortuuian sun began to rise high in the sky, painting the lands with red and gold streaks. On his bare skin it had the curious effect of being absorbed instead of bouncing off or shimmering like it did on mine. I'll have to ask Avrell why that is. Hadrian, like the other morts, is incredibly fit. While he may be younger than the others, he could probably hold his own. Maybe not against Draven or Breccan since they are the biggest dudes around here, but definitely with someone like Oz.

"Like this?" Hadrian asks.

I smile and shout, "That's it. You've got it!"

"Next time, bring Aria," Hadrian suggests, his eyes on the rogcow. "I want to show her what I can do."

Oz and I exchange a knowing look. He talks a lot about Aria. To the point I think he has a serious crush on her. Unfortunately for him, her husband would crush Hadrian if he knew.

"He looks like a wifflebird," Ozias says from beside me, his shoulder-length hair fluttering a bit in the breeze. "So gangly."

"What's a wifflebird?" I ask. One thing I love about living on Mortuus is discovering something new each day. There are always surprises. Sometimes they result in challenges, but with my new family at my side it feels like there isn't anything we can't conquer together.

He scratches his jaw as he thinks. "If a bird and a...leezard?"

"Lizard?" I ask with a smile.

I've been telling him about the different animals on our planet, specifically the ones I've encountered, trying to find similar animals on Mortuus. Kind of like the rogcow is similar to our cows. Just one-eyed and a little creepy. And they...

"Ronnnnk!" Eileen blinks her one eye at Hadrian as though he's annoying her.

"Yes," Oz says with a grin. "If one of your birds mated with a lizard and then was stretched to six feet tall, you'd have the general idea. They flock to the south plain during the warm season, when the geostorms are less violent." He cups a hand around his mouth and shouts, "THEY'RE ALSO THE UGLIEST THING ON MORTUUS!" To me he says, "Not to mention they're not that intelligent. Theron calls them fool birds."

Hadrian, who turns at Oz's shout, merely grins, retrieves his rope, and chases Eileen down for another go. If he's not careful, she'll trample him like she trampled Lox.

It's nice being outside, free of our gear and masks.

Of course, it's pretend outside, but it certainly has the farm feel that makes my heart fuzzy. When Oz built a vacuu-room pen that was virtually all windows and plenty big for Eileen to roam about freely, also equipped with a fan, so she won't get hot, I'd been more than impressed. I swear, these morts are frickin' geniuses.

Hadrian, Oz, and I bonded over building the temporary pen attached to the east side of the facility in the weeks since Draven and I returned. Galen and Theron would've also helped, but they'd gone on an expedition to collect a male rogcow and possibly another female, in addition to gathering more data about the conditions in the cavern we'd discovered. Draven had gone with them after many protests. He hadn't wanted to leave me, not when our own life was growing so rapidly.

As I watch Hadrian and Oz argue, I press a hand to my stomach. Avrell says the baby is growing on schedule. That we're both as healthy as can be, but I still worry. Sometimes I wake up in the middle of the night in the throes of nightmares about our baby being taken like Willow had.

I laugh at myself, pushing the thought from my mind. Not only would the would-be kidnappers have him to reckon with, but all the other morts and their mates too.

My family, all of them, would never let anything happen to us.

"Hadrian, come back." Oz's voice draws me back to reality.

"What is it?" I ask.

"They're back," he says, nodding to the kick of dust. Then I hear the roar of the terrainster.

***

I never thought I'd be the type of woman who relied on anyone else. For as long as I've been alive, I've taken care of myself knowing there was no other way. When Willow was born, I did what I had to do to take care of her, too. I prided myself on my self-reliance.

As I dart through the facility to the decontamination bay, I realize relying on someone else isn't a weakness. Trusting and believing in someone you love makes you stronger together than you are alone.

With Draven, I am stronger.

The doors to the decontamination bay slide open, and he walks through, his minnasuit caked with dust and grime, his helmet dangling from his hand. He's talking with Theron, who practically swaggers through the door, grinning. At the sound of my footsteps slapping against the floor, he looks up.

My heart stumbles in my chest, and maybe I imagine it, but I swear I can feel the baby move. It's probably too early, but a smile splits my face at the thought. When I get close enough, I launch myself into his arms, knocking him back a step.

The scent of antiseptic and something akin to leather fills my nose, but underneath is the spicy reassuring note of Draven. It suffuses my senses and my muscles relax. *Home,* I think. *With him, I'm home.*

"Why don't I get a greeting like that?" Theron complains.

"Don't worry, Theron. When you find your mate, you'll get that and more," Breccan says as he comes to a stop by our side, Aria close beside him as always. Little Sokko is asleep in a sling Oz fashioned for him that Aria wears strapped to her chest. He's a funny looking little thing now that I can look at him without my heart threatening to burst from my chest. Funny looking, but I've grown to love him anyway.

"There are only two women left," he says with a shrug, not meeting anyone's eyes. "Besides, my lady, the *Mayvina,* is all the female I need. Speaking of ships, I'd better check on the terrainsters. I'm sure Galen has ridden his near to broken."

"Will he be all right?" I ask.

Breccan places a hand on my shoulder, but quickly removes it when Draven cracks his neck. "I'll check in on him later. In the meantime, we need to go over what you found in the caves, and we must train, Draven. With the baby and procuring the rogcows it's been weeks since we visited the training room."

Draven only has eyes for me. The heat from them makes me blush. In my head, I start to sing, although it's more of a croon. "Tomorrow," he answers. "Tonight is for my mate."

Breccan begins to speak, but Aria places a quelling hand on his arm. "He just got back from The Graveyard. Let the man rest. Besides, you need to spend some time with your own mate and your son."

We share a very female look and she leads Breccan away, leaving Draven and me alone. I turn back to him and wrap my arms around his muscular shoulders. "I changed my mind. I don't want you to leave me again. I'm an independent woman. I can survive on my own. But I like it better when you're around."

His eyes gleam with possessive pleasure. "My mate missed me," he says.

"Very much," I answer. "Why don't we go back to your quarters, and I can show you how much?"

He nuzzles my throat. "I would like this very much." Sniffing my throat, he groans in pleasure. "I'd forgotten how good you smell. With my seed inside you, they said you'd become more and more attractive. I didn't realize how much."

"Maybe you missed me, too," I tease.

"Why don't *I* show *you*?" He lifts me into his arms in one smooth movement, and I squeal in surprise.

"What are you doing?" I ask.

"Taking you back to our rooms."

"Sugar, I can walk, you know." But he's too busy licking at my throat and trying not to walk into walls to listen. "What's with you?"

"It's the baby. When implantation is successful it makes a female smell intoxicating. Irresistible. The longer mates go without mating, the more the attraction grows. The toxica serves as a nutrient to the growing mortling." His panting breaths puff along my neck as he tries to lick and nibble along my throat.

Giggling, I say, "Watch where you're going, or we'll never get there. Why don't you put me down? We'll get there faster."

His hands tremble where they grip my flesh. "I can't."

By the time we reach his rooms, the need grips me as tight as he does. "Hurry," I urge.

We stumble through the doorway and fall to his bed. He's careful to land in such a way that his arms take all his weight. My hands rake at his suit. "Get this off."

He's aware enough to grin at me. *Grin.* I think back to the man I'd met when I first stumbled out of the cryotube. The one who could barely stomach his own mind. I'm not the only one who's changed.

Maybe I'm his home, too, is my last sane thought before touch, taste, and desire burn away everything but him.

***

"I think we should make training a daily requirement," I say to Aria, who is idly bouncing a slumbering Sokko in her arms. The combination of rogcow milk and colostrum had fattened his cheeks and thighs. Seeing them together is bittersweet. It reminds me of when Willow was a newborn, and I spent hours cycling between being overwhelmed and luminously happy with new motherhood.

Willow.

I begin to hum in my head as I focus back in on the conversation. "We'd have to spin it about protecting the mates and mortlings," I suggest. "Breccan seems like he would go for that. I'm not sure if they'd let us watch all the time, though."

And boy have we been watching them.

Breccan and Draven are evenly matched. Where Breccan is bulkier, Draven is more agile. They're both relentless. Several times I thought one of them would get hurt. But just as they got to that point, they'd break apart.

Right now, they're circling the mats, both of their sub-bones cracking loudly. But it's their outfits—or lack thereof—that have Aria and me so entertained. In an alien version of spandex shorts, our two guys remain topless, and all their yummy muscles are on display. Aria and I giggle like a couple of teenage girls any time we sneak a peek at their giant cocks straining against the fabric. It's so inappropriate, but neither of us is keen on leaving this show. In fact, all we need is for Galen to figure out how to make us popcorn. The mort version, whatever that may be.

Draven and I had spent the night wrapped up in each other. It wasn't until dawn that the cravings abated, and not long after that, Breccan was pounding at our door demanding that Draven join him for training. I tagged along because 1. I missed him, dammit, and 2. Who wouldn't want to watch two half-naked, ripped aliens wrestle?

I sigh. "We'll think of something."

Aria is practically drooling. "It's indecent, really. Maybe I'll talk to Emery once we can tear her away from Galen's greenhouses. She'd *really* enjoy watching Calix participate."

I'm agreeing to this when Sayer sprints through the door, looking alarmed. He spots Aria and me on the sidelines and comes straight to our side.

"What's wrong?" Aria asks.

Sayer's eyes are on me. "You have to come with me. It's urgent. Come now."

I share a panicked look with Aria. "Dammit, Sayer, if Jareth or Theron made a meal out of one of my herd, I'm going to be pissed. I told Draven that I was going to breed some rogcows for meat, but these things take time."

Sayer shakes his head, the top-knot he's tied all his inky black hair in bobbing with the movement. "It's not that. Come, quickly." His nervous energy propels me to my feet, and I bolt after him, leaving Aria and the baby behind.

He leads me down the halls to his office. There's a disembodied voice playing the same transmission over and over on the radio, and it takes a minute for the somewhat familiar voice to penetrate my panicked thoughts.

"My name is Willow Franklin, from Earth II. My mother, Molly, was sentenced to life at the Exilium Penitentiary after killing my father in self-defense. I've been searching for her for twenty years. There are several reformatory planets in our galaxy, but I'm looking for planet Mortuus, formerly known as planet Earth. If you can hear me, please respond."

The message plays again. And again. And again.

Willow.

I can't make sense of it. It's only been a short time, at least for me, but she says she's been looking for me for twenty years. Had I been asleep that long? Had I missed everything?

I crumple to my knees as the transmission repeats. Hope and despair war inside me. Tears of triumph and frustration well up and streak down my cheeks. How is this happening?

Vaguely, I can hear voices behind me, but I strain to listen to the message again, even though I've heard it several times. *Willow*.

"We received the transmission about an hour ago," I can hear Sayer telling the others. "It took me that long to decode it. I remembered Molly saying her daughter's name was Willow. I came to her as soon as I understood."

I sense Draven behind me. He wraps his soothing arms around my waist and lifts me up. Turning to him, I press my face into his chest. "She's here. She's looking for me," I manage.

"We'll find her," he promises. "We're going to find our girl, Molly. This I vow to you."

EPILOGUE
SAYER

EVERYONE IS TALKING ALL AT ONCE, GIVING me a rekking nog-ache. I would ask Avrell for some ghan-dust tablets, but he's in a heated discussion with Calix. Both are growling and baring their fangs, seconds from ripping into each other. Calix has his reasons for not wanting to wake the remaining females, which I completely understand, but we also have Willow to think about.

They may be the key to unlocking everything.

"Enough," Breccan growls, effectively silencing all morts and the two alien females in the room. Even little Sokko grows quiet. The only sound he makes is suckling on his mother's nipple. "I've heard your argument, Calix, and your worry is valid. Emery nearly lost her life when she was pulled from the cryotube."

Calix wraps a protective arm around his mate. She's come a long way since then, when Aria foolishly yanked her out of cryosleep before she was ready. However, Emery came with health issues. It wasn't all Aria's fault. I think he fails to remember that part.

"But it must be done. We cannot keep those two alien humans the way they are forever. We morts are just, good, and kind. We are not Kevins, which is why we cannot keep them caged and asleep any longer." He frowns and gives Avrell a nod. "Check their vitals then wake them. Emery and Calix will assist. Their discovery with the toxica agents could be useful if these aliens also have health issues." The three of them leave without further argument.

Then, he points to me. "Sayer, I want you to continue attempting to reach Willow. I'm sure Molly will want to assist, as will Draven. It's imperative that you make contact with her."

Of course I will. As our faction's linguistics specialist, communication and language is my job. If there's a way to speak to her, I'll find it. "On it," I affirm. "Right, Uvie?" I tug my hair out of its knot, and it cascades down my front. With a quick twist, I affix it to the top of my head again—like Aria taught me—which is purposeful for keeping it out of my way while I work.

"Correct," Uvie chirps from the overhead speakers. "I'm scanning the transmission for locator pings."

"The *Mayvina* is purring like a baby sabrevipe, Brec," Theron says, bouncing with his usual energy. "You've been wanting Hadrian to learn to pilot, and we should patrol from the skies. This knocks two items off our list."

Breccan grumbles but gives a nod that has Hadrian flinging up his rogstud horns and hooting with excitement.

Jareth catches my stare from across the table and smirks. He's been fiddling with his piece of metal for weeks now. A piece that has Draven practically running at the mere sight of it. I lift my brow at him as though to ask, *What are you going to do with that thing?*

He rolls it across the table to me, and I catch it in the palm of my hand just as it rolls off the table. I shake my head at him. Rekk no. I know what this ring is for, and that's his thing, not mine. My cock is too nice to willingly run a thick, metal hoop through the tip of it.

"Jareth and Oz," Breccan says, causing Jareth to straighten to attention. "Help Aria make sure the subfaction is ready for our new aliens. See to it that my mate has what she needs to welcome them properly."

He shouts out more orders to the other morts, and

soon, we're off on our missions. Jareth bumps his shoulder to mine as we walk down the corridor, grabbing my attention.

"You think the last two females will know more than Molly and the other awoken aliens?" he asks, his brows furrowing together. His choppy black hair is wrecked today, and I have the urge to help smooth it out some.

I shrug and let out a sigh. "Not sure. Each alien has known more than the last. If there's any information they can offer, we could rekking use it. We have to find Willow."

Jareth scowls. "So Breccan can force one of us to mate with her, too?"

Screeching to a halt, I poke him in the chest, but the giant mort doesn't move. "He won't *make* anyone do anything they don't want to do. There are plenty of other morts around here desperate for a chance to mate with one of the alien females."

He seems to calm with my reassurance.

"You never gave me my ring back," he says, his lips lifting up on one side.

I pat my pockets and feign confusion. "Must have lost it."

"I could pierce you," he offers, his black eyes gleaming wickedly.

"You could rekking try," I growl, giving him a shove.

He laughs and walks backward, making sure to make horrifying gestures pretending to do said piercing that have me shuddering. "I want my ring back later. Find it, Say."

Ignoring him, I storm over to my comms room where Molly sits in Draven's lap. They're sitting there tense as can be while they listen to the same transmission over and over again.

"Anything new?" I ask.

"No," Draven grumbles.

"How many times have you listened to the same transmission?" My eyes dart between them. Molly's shoulders slump, and Draven won't make eye contact with me. Clearly the entire time I've been in my meeting.

"Fifty-seven times," Uvie chirps.

My brows lift, and Draven grumbles.

"Tattletale," Molly huffs.

I let out a heavy sigh. "You look exhausted, Molly. Why don't you let Draven take you back to your quarters, and get some rest? I promise I will notify you the moment I know anything."

She frowns and opens her mouth like she might argue, but Draven must agree with me because he's already standing with her in his arms. "Thank you," she utters a moment before Draven stalks away with her.

Once the door closes behind them, I relax. It's difficult to work with them staring at me. I busy myself for the next couple of hours, reading through Uvie's data on the screen concerning the pings on the transmission as I attempt to triangulate a location. The pings are scattered. At first, it appears as though the vessel Willow is on is moving. But then, I realize it's a mask covering a location. The pings, I quickly uncover, are in a pattern. I tap away on my computer, trying some different calculations to see if anything begins to make sense. Since there are easily thousands of pings, I run a command for Uvie to work through them using my calculations. If there's a pattern, we're going to discover it. Then we'll be able to pinpoint exactly where she is.

From there, I'm not sure what will happen.

The door slides open and Jareth rushes in, his chest heaving.

"What?" I demand, panic rising up inside of me.

"I don't know," he pants. "Avrell said to come get you. It's an emergency."

I'm out of my chair and bounding after him in the next moment. We rush down the corridor, our boots pounding on the floor resounding around us. He whips out his keycard, and the door to the Avrell's lab slides open.

Screaming. All that can be heard is mad, female ranting like she's got a case of The Rades.

"—hell no! Hell no, freaks. This is not happening!"

Jareth comes to a screeching halt just inside the doorway, and I bump into him. Peering over his shoulder with my palm pressed at his lower back, I take in the scene. On one table, an alien human remains sleeping despite having been pulled from her cryotube. The other one, though...

She's feral.

Despite wearing one of the medical gowns, she's anything but weak or sick. This alien is fierce and furious. Despite being two nogs shorter than Avrell, she points up at him with her filed down claw like it has the power to flay him like a magknife. Avrell's jaw clenches as he bites back words.

"I know it's a lot to take in," Emery tries. "But if—"

"No," the feral female growls. "I've heard this three times already. You want to take me to something called the sub-faction. Everyone is nice. Who cares if they're big fucking freaks because you all want to have their babies. Yeah, got all that." She seethes with rage, her long, dark, brown hair swishing back and forth with her movement. "The part I'm not getting is how this one"—she pokes Avrell in the chest—"says I'm fucking pregnant!"

Jareth stiffens. I meet Calix's stare, and his jaw clenches.

Pregnant?

"Listen, honey," Emery starts again.

"Grace. My name isn't honey or alien," she snarls, her words directed at Avrell. "It's Grace Miller. AND I AM A FUCKING VIRGIN! My name isn't Mary and this guy here isn't God! This is not happening!"

"She's pregnant," Jareth mutters, his voice a mixture of fear and awe.

As though she's a geostorm chasing the sun from our world, she slowly turns around, darkness burning from eyes the same color as Jareth's cock ring. Dark silver. Strong. Piercing.

Rekk.

"She is pregnant," Calix agrees, finding his voice. "And the mortling belongs to you."

Jareth freezes and shakes his head in disbelief. But Calix isn't looking at him. His intense stare is on me. I peel my eyes from his to scan down her body. Her stomach isn't as big as Emery's, but it's swollen. Obviously so.

Rekk no.

Rekk no.

Rekk no.

"Yeah, you've said that," Grace hisses. "Three times."

I wince, realizing I said it out loud.

She walks our way, and her steely eyes burn with fury, melting me with just one look. "*You* did this to me?"

I blink at her, understanding her meaning. As though I pushed myself on her while she slept. "I, uh—"

She smacks me right across the face, the burn from her hard hit shocking me. Jareth growls at her, his sub-bones snapping out of control. Rekking great. Calix makes a grab for Grace's arm just as I step in front of Jareth, blocking him from attacking her. His chest bumps my back.

"We ought to toss you in a reform cell," Jareth bites out at her.

"Toss *him* in while you're at it!" she cries out. "Where I come from, we don't allow rapists to walk free!"

"No," I argue. "We are not Kevins. I would never."

"No one physically violated you," Avrell assures her. "I was the one to inseminate the females."

She turns her fury back to him. And as he rattles

off all the specifics of what he did, she seems to deflate. Where Jareth and I are unknowing about medicines and biological code, this female seems to understand him clearly.

"Come on, Grace," Emery says. "Just us. Let's go. I'll take you somewhere, so you can eat something and catch your breath. I'm so sorry."

This time, Grace seems to see reason. She allows Emery to tug her away. But before she gets past us, Grace stops to narrow her eyes at me.

"I may have your alien bastard baby inside me, but I'm not a monster. I can feel it kicking." Her hard eyes seem to flicker with a softness before it's chased away again by anger. "The poor thing is innocent. But don't think for one second that I'll let you be some deadbeat dad. If I'm forced into this, you will be too. Got it, freak?"

All I can do is nod.

Because what the rekk else am I supposed to do?

She's pregnant with *my* mortling.

Mine.

Pride and mortification war back and forth inside me. I'll allow myself time later to understand what this will mean and how it will impact my life.

Now is not the time.

Jareth storms out of the lab, and I shoot Avrell an

apologetic look before trotting after him. It's not until we're within his quarters that he reveals what's going on inside that nog of his.

The door closes behind me, and I slowly approach him.

"Jareth..."

He turns and glowers at me, but I don't miss the hurt glimmering in his black eyes. "These aliens have ruined everything."

I shake my head vehemently. "No, they haven't. They've given our people hope."

He winces. I soften the blow of my words by tenderly touching his cheek.

"I can father this mortling, but I won't ever mate with her," I vow. "I already have a mate." Reaching into my pocket, I pull out his cock ring. "And if my mate is done pouting, I'd like for him to show me his cock that's clearly missing its ring."

His gaze drops to my mouth. "I'll feed myself to a sabrevipe if you willingly bed her," he says dramatically. "Go to The Eternals without you."

I chuckle and grip his cock through his suit. It's hard and strains against the material. "You're not going anywhere without me. You've been my mate—albeit in secret—for six revolutions, Jare. You think I'm going to give you up now?"

He lets out a hiss of air when I rub at him more forcefully, his hand that's always cut from working with metal grasping my wrist. "If they find out—"

But they won't. They never do. We're careful.

What we're doing with each other is unheard of among our people. Something so taboo, it cannot be voiced. But when you're hopeless and lonely, sometimes your heart gives you something you desperately need. With Jareth, we fill a void in each other I certainly don't intend on interfering with. I need him, and he needs me.

"Our secret." I run my lips along his, our breaths mingling together. "We're solid. This female can't change that."

His hand slides to the back of my neck, and his nog rests against mine. "I really wish I could believe that."

"Jareth..." I growl.

The argument is no longer up for discussion because he silences me with his mouth. And then later, from my knees, I make him bellow with mine.

Nothing will tear us apart.

Especially not some alien female.

Even if she *is* carrying our future in her womb...

Keep reading with the next installment...
THE UNCERTAIN SCIENTIST!

ACKNOWLEDGMENTS

K WEBSTER

Thank you to my husband for always being so supportive. I love you, boo.

A big giant thank you to Nicole Blanchard for taking this journey into the unknown right along with me. Each time we get to nerd out over our world, my heart swells. I've enjoyed writing every single one of these books with you and can't wait to write many more! I rekking love you!

A huge thank you to my Krazy for K Webster's Books reader group. You all are insanely supportive and I can't thank you enough. I love when y'all get Krazy with me and read things you wouldn't normally read because you're curious like me!

A gigantic thank you to those who helped me with this book. Elizabeth Clinton, Ella Stewart, Misty Walker, Holly Sparks, Rosa Saucedo, Jillian Ruize, Kim BookJunkie, and Gina Behrends—you ladies are my rock!

A big thank you to my author friends who have given me your friendship and your support. You have no idea how much that means to me.

Thank you to all of my blogger friends both big and small that go above and beyond to always share my stuff. You all rock! #AllBlogsMatter

Emily A. Lawrence, thank you SO much for editing this book. You're a rock star and I can't thank you enough! Love you!

A big thanks to Indie Sage PR for pimping us out!

Lastly but certainly not least of all, thank you to all of the wonderful readers out there who are willing to hear my story and enjoy my characters like I do. It means the world to me!

NICOLE BLANCHARD

To Afton, thank you always for being my favorite person in the whole world.

I cannot say enough good things about working with K. Thank you for your motivation (and gentle nagging), for pushing me to be a better writer. Thank you for loving aliens as much as I do. Thank you for being a wonderful person.

To Mr. Wonderful, for supporting and cheering me on even when I'm neurotic and silly. I can't thank you enough for everything.

A huge thank you to the girls in Nicole's Knock-outs for motivating me each day to keep working and writing. I can't tell you how much it means to me to have you in my corner.

To the team who bring a book from production to publication including, but not limited to, IndieSage PR, editor Emily A. Lawrence, and the countless book bloggers and bookstagrammers THANK YOU!

ABOUT K WEBSTER

K Webster is a *USA Today Bestselling author.* Her titles have claimed many bestseller tags in numerous categories, are translated in multiple languages, and have been adapted into audiobooks. She lives in "Tornado Alley" with her husband, two children, and her baby dog named Blue. When she's not writing, she's reading, drinking copious amounts of coffee, and researching aliens.

facebook.com/authorkwebster

twitter.com/KristiWebster

instagram.com/authorkwebster

amazon.com/K-Webster

bookbub.com/authors/k-webster

goodreads.com/K_Webster

ALSO BY K WEBSTER

Psychological Romance Standalones:

My Torin

Whispers and the Roars

Cold Cole Heart

Blue Hill Blood

Romantic Suspense Standalones:

Dirty Ugly Toy

El Malo

Notice

Sweet Jayne

The Road Back to Us

Surviving Harley

Love and Law

Moth to a Flame

Erased

Extremely Forbidden Romance Standalones:

The Wild

Hale

Like Dragonflies

Taboo Treats:

Bad Bad Bad

Coach Long

Ex-Rated Attraction

Mr. Blakely

Easton

Crybaby

Lawn Boys

Malfeasance

Renner's Rules

The Glue

Dane

Enzo

Red Hot Winter

Dr. Dan

KKinky Reads Collection:

Share Me

Choke Me

Daddy Me

Watch Me

Hurt Me

Contemporary Romance Standalones:

Wicked Lies Boys Tell

The Day She Cried

Untimely You

Heath

Sundays are for Hangovers

A Merry Christmas with Judy

Zeke's Eden

Schooled by a Senior

Give Me Yesterday

Sunshine and the Stalker

Bidding for Keeps

B-Sides and Rarities

Paranormal Romance Standalones:

Apartment 2B

Running Free

Mad Sea

War & Peace Series:

This is War, Baby (Book 1)

This is Love, Baby (Book 2)

This Isn't Over, Baby (Book 3)

This Isn't You, Baby (Book 4)

This is Me, Baby (Book 5)

This Isn't Fair, Baby (Book 6)

This is the End, Baby (Book 7 – a novella)

Lost Planet Series:

The Forgotten Commander (Book 1)

The Vanished Specialist (Book 2)

The Mad Lieutenant (Book 3)

The Uncertain Scientist (Book 4)

The Lonely Orphan (Book 5)

2 Lovers Series:

Text 2 Lovers (Book 1)

Hate 2 Lovers (Book 2)

Thieves 2 Lovers (Book 3)

Pretty Little Dolls Series:

Pretty Stolen Dolls (Book 1)

Pretty Lost Dolls (Book 2)

Pretty New Doll (Book 3)

Pretty Broken Dolls (Book 4)

The V Games Series:

Vlad (Book 1)

Ven (Book 2)

Vas (Book 3)

Four Fathers Books:

Pearson

Four Sons Books:

Camden

Elite Seven Books:

Gluttony

Greed

Not Safe for Amazon Books:

The Wild

Hale

Bad Bad Bad

This is War, Baby

Like Dragonflies

The Breaking the Rules Series:

Broken (Book 1)

Wrong (Book 2)

Scarred (Book 3)

Mistake (Book 4)

Crushed (Book 5 – a novella)

The Vegas Aces Series:

Rock Country (Book 1)

Rock Heart (Book 2)

Rock Bottom (Book 3)

The Becoming Her Series:

Becoming Lady Thomas (Book 1)

Becoming Countess Dumont (Book 2)

Becoming Mrs. Benedict (Book 3)

Alpha & Omega Duet:

Alpha & Omega (Book 1)

Omega & Love (Book 2)

ABOUT NICOLE BLANCHARD

Nicole Blanchard is the *New York Times* and *USA Today* best-selling author of gritty romantic suspense and heartwarming new adult romance. She and her family reside in the south along with their menagerie of pets. Visit her website www.authornicoleblanchard.com for more information or to subscribe to her newsletter for updates on sales and new releases. P.S. there's also a free book!

facebook.com/authornicoleblanchard

twitter.com/blanchardbooks

instagram.com/authornicoleblanchard

amazon.com/author/nicoleblanchard

bookbub.com/authors/nicole-blanchard

goodreads.com/nicole_blanchard

ALSO BY NICOLE BLANCHARD

First to Fight Series

Anchor

Warrior

Survivor

Savior

Honor

Box Set: Books 1-5

Traitor

Operator

Aviator

Captor

Protector

Friend Zone Series

Friend Zone

Frenemies

Friends with Benefits

The Lost Planet Series

The Forgotten Commander

The Vanished Specialist

The Mad Lieutenant

Immortals Ever After Series

Deal with a Dragon

Vow to a Vampire

Fated to a Fae King

Dark Romance

Toxic

Fatal

Standalone Novellas

Bear with Me

Darkest Desires

Mechanical Hearts

Made in the USA
Lexington, KY
23 October 2019